GAFF*

* A sharp piercing or cutting instrument fastened
to the leg of a gamecock in cockfighting.

GAFF

SHAN CORREA

Ω
Published by
PEACHTREE PUBLISHERS
1700 Chattahoochee Avenue
Atlanta, Georgia 30318-2112

www.peachtree-online.com

Cover design by Maureen Withee
Book design by Melanie McMahon Ives

Printed in February 2010 by Lake Book Manufacturing in Melrose Park, Illinois, in the United States of America
10 9 8 7 6 5 4 3 2 1
First Edition

Library of Congress Cataloging-in-Publication Data

Correa, E. Shan.
Gaff / written by Shan Correa.
p. cm.
Summary: In Hawaii, thirteen-year-old Paul Silva is determined to find a way to get his family out of the illegal cockfighting business.
ISBN 978-1-56145-526-3
[1. Cockfighting–Fiction. 2. Roosters–Fiction. 3. Animal rescue–Fiction. 4. Conduct of life–Fiction 5. Hawaii–Fiction.] I. Title.
PZ7.C8159Gf 2010
[Fic]–dc22

2009024508

To my super Hawaii guys,
Les and our sons Evan and Brandon

ONE

Only five kids—no, six—have ever slept over at my house: Brian Harada, Kia Simpson, Junior Reeves, Damien Kekau, my second cousin Marty Silva who moved to the mainland last year, and Angel "Sal" Salvador. And only one kid slept over more than once.

We've called Angel "Sal" for as long as I can remember because "Angel" didn't sound like a real name to us. Maybe because none of the rest of us were Filipino. Besides, "Angel" didn't fit him very well. Anyway, Sal Salvador's the only kid who ever spent more than one night at my house.

You think maybe my house is old or smelly or haunted or something? No way! It's nice—pretty big, and not too messy. And I'm lucky because I have my own room and it's in back where it's cool.

But my friends won't stay here at night on account of the birds and all the racket they make, especially really early in the morning. Rooster #43 starts them out with the crowing. I know: I got up at three in the morning last week to find out who started all the commotion. I know a lot of the birds, and #43 is this squawky, smallish year-old guy with a long neck.

Good for crowing. So I wasn't totally surprised when, about three-fifteen, he let out with a crow that about knocked me on my *okole!*

He woke up every chicken in his neighborhood and they crowed until the sun came up at six, when normal roosters are supposed to say it's time to wake up. I'd gone back to bed way before then. Went right back to sleep, even with all the racket going on. I couldn't do that when we first got the roosters, but now it's easy.

Kids who don't raise roosters never sleep over more than one time, though. Junior Reeves lives on a farm farther up the mountain and has tons of animals, but even he said that one night here was enough.

Junior's only lived in Hawaii a couple of years, but he's already picked up lots of the things we do here in Hawaii. If you'd seen him even a week after he got here, he'd flash you a *shaka* sign. And now he speaks perfect Hawaiian pidgin. My parents don't like me to speak pidgin because they say it will limit me in school and in real life. So most of the time, I speak pretty good English. Standard English, they call it in school. Then I can switch when I'm with my friends who talk pidgin, so it works out fine.

Anyway, when the roosters woke Junior up that time, he said something like, "Neva again, Paulie! Neva, eva aks me stay at you house. *Noisy,* da buggas! Sound like sireens all night. Like banshees, da cheekins. Sheesh! Gotta be *pupule* to sleep tru all dat."

Not true. Sal sleeps in the other twin bed in my room just fine, and he's not crazy. But then, he grew up with roosters.

His family raised them for years before my dad started. Ours are on three acres in front of our house, so they're not close to my bedroom, but Sal's dad lets the birds stay just any old place they want. They sleep under the car in the carport sometimes, and once they chased a poor mongoose right into Mrs. Salvador's kitchen. My dad always says that Mr. Salvador's a good breeder, but not much competition. He never has more than forty gamecocks at a time, and he's not very organized.

We have over two hundred, which tells you why there's so much noise. Two hundred big, loudmouth birds all screeching at once sometimes. Well, I guess you just have to get used to it. And it's worse when I stay over at Sal's. You'll be sound asleep, and a loose bird will hop up on his window frame and "Er-uh-Er-uh-*Errr!*" And even Sal and me just about fall out of bed, they scare us so much—or at least we fall off his mattress, which is on the floor, so really we wouldn't get very hurt if we did fall out. But what Junior said in his best pidgin was true. The roosters are super noisy little buggas!

But roosters are what we do, how we earn our living. Dad breeds and raises strong, healthy birds, then he sells them for hundreds—sometimes even thousands—of dollars when they're about two years old. And even if most of my friends won't sleep over here, that's okay. I love these noisy guys.

That's probably why I invited Honey Kealoha up to my house this morning. She'd never been here before, and of course she'd never slept over because she was a girl. So I really wanted to just show her around. Show off our birds.

But the first thing she said when we stood on our front

lanai and looked out over the rows of my dad's roosters was, "This reminds me of death."

She said it real quiet, but I wouldn't have been more surprised if she'd screamed it in my ear. I looked down at her hands, holding onto the wooden railing. They held on tight, like she thought she might fall down onto our front grass.

"Death?" I said. "Something here reminds you of death?"

"It's just a feeling, Paul." She swung her arm around and pointed from one side of our lawn to the other. "What do you see here?"

"Our grass, I guess. Our lawn here by the lanai. Then our beautiful roosters, all of them in the shade now. Every bird in his own little A-frame cottage so the sun doesn't cook him when it's hot like this. My mom's little garden over there."

Honey nodded. "Yeah. That's what I see, too."

"Then... *death?*"

"I know that's weird. Maybe it reminds me of a cemetery. All the rows nice and neat, with grass between them like at Punchbowl, the cemetery that's up above Honolulu. Did you ever go there?"

I didn't want to tell her that I'd only been off our island once in my life, and that was to Kauai, not Oahu. So I just said, "No. But I've seen it on the reruns of *Hawaii 5-0.* You know those pictures at the beginning? Dad said they took them at Punchbowl Crater. That's where my Grampa Landers is. He died in Vietnam when my mom was little."

"I'm sorry."

"That's okay. If you have to be in a cemetery, Punchbowl is a pretty good place to be, I guess."

"Well, it looks kind of like this when you're there inside the crater. With long, neat rows of grave markers. One for every grave. Every soldier. Maybe that's why I get this sad feeling here."

"Yeah."

"Or I'm sad when I see the roosters. Knowing that someday—"

"Hey! Don't feel sorry for these birds. They have the best life ever, you know! Dad and Uncle Porky treat these birds with *respect.* Everybody says we have the best birds on the island. You should see what we feed them. Nothing but the best. The best food we can buy." I pointed to the low white building on our right. "See that? That's the infirmary. A little hospital, just for the chickens. Anybody gets sick, my uncle takes care of them right there. He takes care of them like, like..."

"Treasures?"

"Sure. These guys closest to the house will be sold pretty soon. Uncle Porky has trained them at his place and they're ready for the buyers now. This is how Dad supports Mom and Emily and me since he got hurt at the lumberyard almost two years ago."

"That was so terrible." She shut her eyes for a second.

"Yeah. I don't even like to think about it. Don't worry, though. He's a lot better now."

"Oh. Good." She looked around like she was thinking about something else. "What happens if a bird is, you know...injured?"

"Infirmary. My Uncle Porky's the best chicken doctor in Hawaii."

I had Honey follow me down the steps then, and did what I'd planned to do for about a hundred years: showed her around. Showed her our birds, their beautiful feathers and wide wings. Honey said they had clear, wise-looking eyes, and I told her not to get too close. They can really peck, you know.

Honey pointed at some of the older birds. "Those roosters over there don't have any combs and…what are those reddish, wobbly things under their chins called?"

"Wattles," I said. "They were dubbed—trimmed off—a few months ago because they aren't necessary. Don't worry. Uncle Porky does it so it doesn't hurt them."

We ducked into the infirmary. "Wow," Honey said. "It even smells like a hospital in here."

"Yeah. The disinfectant. Everything spic and span, my mom says. Everything clean and nice."

Nobody was inside—no Uncle Porky or Dad. No birds recovering from injuries. I was kinda happy about that. Seeing a hurt bird might make Honey want to leave. She's a girl, after all, and maybe she isn't as brave as I thought she was. But she didn't seem so sad now. I think she was beginning to get impressed.

When I showed her the incubators with the baby chicks, she smiled and watched them wiggle around. Some had just hatched and were super ugly. She didn't even care.

Next, we went out of the infirmary to see where our brood hens lived in a small chicken house. They had a big fenced-off yard where they were pecking and clucking around.

Honey laughed when she spotted a fat Miner Blue hen in

the yard. "It looks like that girl's taking a bath in the dirt and dust!"

"That's just what she's doing. Looks fun?"

"Not really. Guess I've never seen anyone take a bath so they can get dirty. About how many hens are here?"

"Never more than twenty. They're special types, used mostly for breeding, not for eggs. We do have eggs for breakfast, though. We can give you some if you want."

After our tour, I took Honey up the hill to the back of the house. It's shady there, with a little lawn and a grove of bamboo and octopus trees and woodrose vines back behind. Ferns and *ohia* trees hang onto the lava rock behind that.

"We have a better view from the front lanai," I said, "but it's okay back here."

"I like it here." She wiped some woodrose leaves off the old green picnic table bench and slid in, facing the ferns and the trees. While she couldn't see me, I tried to push my awful hair down because I knew it was all wild. Then I sat down on the same bench, but way over to the other end. My crazy cat Milo jumped up on the bench, too, right beside Honey. He curled up and let her pet him, just like she lived here or something.

"So this is Milo," Honey said, bending over him and rubbing the back of his ears.

"Yeah. I forgot you never met him."

"No, but you talk about him so much, I feel like I know him. Hey, Milo. You're a beautiful cat, aren't you?" She petted him some more and he closed his eyes. "I see why you named him that," she said to me. "He's exactly the color of *milo* wood."

"That's why I decided on the name. Some people say it wrong, though, if they're not from here. I wrote his name, 'Milo,' on the vet's papers when we got him and the lady who worked there said his name My-low instead of Mee-low. I had to tell her about the wood."

Honey smiled. "He's really pretty, Paul. He's always friendly like this?"

"He usually doesn't like people very much. Me, maybe, because I feed him. But most of the time, he's not sure if he even likes *me.* I don't think he's gone near a girl since Emily dressed him up in her doll's muumuu and carted him around in her doll stroller. I'm kinda surprised he's doing that."

"Doing what?"

"Purring. Going to sleep snuggled up there."

She giggled when Milo came out with this super loud purr. "I really like it out here, in back of your house."

"Oh, yeah. Right. It's okay here. Cooler. But in front, you can see the roosters, then clear down to the ocean if it isn't foggy or raining. If you have good eyes like me, you can see container ships and those big cruise ships, even. You could probably see a tsunami coming, but we're up too high to get flooded. Your house is out of the tidal wave zone, too, right?"

"Uh-huh. But not as high up in the hills as you guys."

"Yeah. We like it here. My mom and dad bought it about a month before my dad got hurt. We have over three acres."

I stopped myself from bragging any more and said, "Be back in a second." I scooted off the bench and went in the back door to the kitchen. I'd checked the fridge before

Honey came so I knew we had two Pepsis in there. I grabbed them and took some of those big Hilo Saloon Pilots crackers out in back. We ate them and talked, mostly about old friends and stuff. We were laughing about Mr. Matayoshi, our second-grade teacher, when we heard a couple of honks.

"That's Dad," Honey said. "He's picking me up and we're going fishing. I'll take him a cracker if it's okay."

"Oh. Sure." We both got up and headed around to Mr. Kealoha's big Ford pickup. The door was open, and Honey climbed aboard. "*Mahalo*, Paul," she said politely from the rolled-down window.

"Sure. You're welcome."

"It was really interesting coming here today. It was nice."

I waved to her, watched the truck back down the drive, and then she was gone. After standing there for a minute, I went back to the picnic table, where there was no Honey and no Milo. I finished up my Saloon Pilots, chewing them real slow and wondering why Honey said that coming over was "interesting," and not "awesome."

I shouldn't have been surprised, I guess. I shouldn't have been surprised about anything that had to do with Honey Kealoha. I'd known her since small-kid-time, and she always said whatever she felt. We were both in Mrs. Lau's kindergarten class, and even though we hadn't been in the same class since second grade, we're both in Mrs. Chong's seventh grade class now and we're kinda catching up with each other again.

Hardly anybody knows Honey's real name is Malia. Even the teachers call her Honey. She was Honey in kindergarten even. And she was cute. She had honey-colored skin, like now, and long, black, shiny hair with a *pua* clipped behind her ear. Every day a different pua. A red hibiscus from the Kealohas' hedge, or maybe a peach-colored flower from their huge old plumeria tree.

I don't remember a lot about kindergarten because it was so long ago, but I do remember that Honey was there. Sometimes my mom let her mom pick us up after school, and Honey and me would climb the plumeria tree or their tall mango tree. But that was just when the mangos weren't blooming, because I'm allergic, and even when I was five I already had huge sneezing fits when the mangos were flowering.

Even then Honey was always honest, and that could be a real pain. I should've known she might be bothered about seeing our fighting roosters.

* * *

I was rinsing off the cracker plate in the kitchen when the phone by the sink rang. I almost dropped the dish—I always jump when that stupid phone rings. It's an old-fashioned wall phone and you can't make the ringer any quieter. I grabbed it with my wet hands before it could ring again.

"Howzit?" the voice said.

"I knew it was you, Sal."

Sal and I have this thing. We almost always know when we're thinking about each other. Maybe that's because we've been best friends forever. But I was still surprised when he asked me if Honey just left my house.

"How'd you know?"

"I saw her dad's blue truck go by from your direction and took a wild guess. What, you think I'm psychic or something?"

"Yeah, she was here. I showed her around." I wondered for a second if I should say more. "She acted kind of weird when she was here."

"Like how?"

"I don't think she liked the roosters."

"She's a girl, Paulie. What did you expect?"

"Well. I sure didn't think she'd look around and be thinking about *death*."

"Death?"

"Death. Cemeteries. What happens to the birds who get hurt in the cockfights. That kinda thing."

I thought Sal might laugh, but when he finally talked again, he was serious.

"Paulie," he said, "you're smart, but you always miss the easy stuff. The obvious stuff. Honey's mom died this year. Of course that's on her mind. This probably had nothing to do with you or the roosters."

I thought for a second. Then I realized he was right. Why was I so dense? With anybody else, I'd have understood right away, but Honey sometimes makes me block out all my common sense. Just because she never talks about losing her mom doesn't mean she doesn't think about her all the time.

I remember how bad I felt when my dad's aunt, my Great-auntie Sylvana, died last year. She was like a grandmother to me, always spoiling me and my sister. Making quilts for us, knitting sweaters. She showed my mom how to make this great Portuguese sweet bread, and every time we have it I miss her. I can't even imagine what it would be like to have my own mom or dad die.

Mrs. Kealoha was a great mom, and Honey really loved her. Honey's strong, though. And brave, for a girl. So she probably just didn't want me to know what she was feeling this time.

"Paulie?" Sal asked. "You still there?"

"Oh. Yeah. Just thinking. You're probably right about Honey's mom and all. So...you coming over?"

"Nah. I don't think so. Wanna come over here? We should get started on the science thing."

"Is anybody at home?"

Again, Sal knew exactly what I was thinking. "By anybody, you mean my brother?"

"Yeah. I guess...Raymond's home?"

"He took off in his van for Waiele right after I got up this morning. He won't be back until tomorrow night. And Mom and Dad are down at St. Ann's for something all day, them and Eggie Fernandez's mom and dad. A church planning retreat or something like that. So come on over. The coast is clear."

"Okay. In a little while."

"See ya...and Paulie? Roosters are a man's thing, that's all. At least in my family. My mom won't have anything to do with um. Just ignore Honey. So. Laters."

TWO

I did a few things—got rid of the spam from my e-mail, checked on the birds, took off my good aloha shirt and put on my "Get Poi?" T-shirt—before I took the two-minute walk over to Sal's. We're both at the end of our road, and the Salvadors are only one house over, but we can't just yell across at each other or anything. His house is a little ways over on the other side of the trees and we both have these really long driveways. Sal and me talk about clearing a path between our houses, but it's too jungley—too thick with trees and plants. We'd also have to build a bridge over the stream there.

At Sal's, I pretty much forgot about the whole Honey thing because we had work to do. We were partners for the science fair project and we needed to come up with some ideas. Which we finally did. Mrs. Chong had told us to choose something we knew about. "That'll give you a head start," she said.

The one thing Sal and I knew a *lot* about was the birds. We decided to do an experiment about culling roosters, which is what our dads do to breed stronger, better birds. They keep and breed only the best of the birds that hatch.

We got the general idea down in Sal's computer. The whole thing took almost an hour, and because we'd been thinking and working so hard, we decided to reward ourselves with something more fun. We hiked along the stream to the big pond that's uphill from our houses.

It had gotten even hotter. The trade winds had died down to where we were pretty sweaty by the time we crawled over the rocks and waded into the pool.

"Oh, man!" I screamed. "This isn't water. It's ice!"

"Yeah! It feels *so* great!"

Sal was already up to his neck in the clear water, and he dog-paddled across the pool. We splashed and dive-bombed each other just like little kids.

"Lucky we live Hawaii, uh?" I said when we stretched out on a giant blue Bank of Hawaii beach towel and let the sun dry us off.

Sal said, "You got it. Lucky we live Hawaii! Ummm." And he yawned and I yawned, and I knew that for a while at least, I had no worries. About Honey, about science class, nothing. Everything was warm and peaceful, except for one crazy Brazilian cardinal who every now and then let out with this long, really complicated song. I don't think he was talking to anybody, just singing away for the heck of it, and I liked his song.

* * *

I think I was dreaming about being at the pool in the middle of the night when I heard somebody say "Paul!" It was my dad's voice, close to the bed, and I was wide-awake by the time he called me again.

"Paul. Come with me." He turned on my bedroom light before he went out the door. I scrambled out of bed and pulled on my pants and followed him as quick as I could. When his voice sounds like that, I don't ask questions. I know something's wrong. Something big.

Dad can't walk too fast since the accident at Nakasone's Lumberyard where he used to work. He was in a wheelchair for weeks after a load of lumber shifted and fell on him and crushed his right foot and hurt his back. For a while he had to use a walker, but now, almost two years later, he just needs a cane. I caught up with him before he'd gotten down the front steps.

He had his rifle in his right hand and he handed it to me while we walked. I took it, but my stomach started to feel scared.

Dad didn't turn on the lights outside, but the moon was really bright. I could hear the roosters over in the farthest part of the yard. They weren't crowing, but there were noises. A lot of commotion.

Even before I saw it, I guessed.

"A pig?" I whispered, and saw Dad nod as he walked ahead.

That was bad. But good, too—we weren't going out in the dark looking for a person, at least. Somebody poaching our birds.

But then I saw it. A huge black shape. A wild boar, snuffling and rummaging around while the roosters panicked and squawked. The birds couldn't get away because they were tethered to stakes. All they could do was screech and run around in circles.

I started running toward the boar. I passed Dad, and before he caught up with me, I saw the pig close in front of me. It was gigantic! Bigger than any I'd seen, even the dead ones Uncle Porky brought back from hunting. But this guy was alive! He smelled terrible, and I couldn't believe he was that close to me. What if he charged? His huge tusks could toss me around like one of Emily's dolls.

I cocked the rifle. "Should I try to shoot it?" I asked Dad, my voice all shaky. My arm was all shaky, too.

Dad didn't hear me because of the roosters' squawking and boar's snuffling, or else he just didn't answer, but by then there wasn't any need for shooting because the boar took off, letting out a crazy squeal. His legs looked little, but boy, could he move! By the time Dad said no, don't shoot, the guy was clear back in the trees again. Over the rooster noise, I could hear him shattering branches and stomping down tree ferns.

"Wow!" I said. "That guy was *gigantic!* Do you think he killed any of our birds?"

"No more than you killed *him,* I guess," Dad said. I could tell by his voice that he was smiling even though he was in front of me then, checking out the roosters and calming them down. I uncocked the rifle and put it down so I could help him. Finally everybody was okay, and we waited to see if the pig would come back.

"What are we going to do, Dad?" I asked.

"Well, we have to keep him from returning, that's the main thing. We've been lucky so far, but it's time we build a fence. Hate to do it, but we're going to need to stretch two or three lengths of barbed wire all around the birds."

"Mom won't like that. It won't look nice by her garden."

"Has to be done. She'll understand. It may be just a temporary thing, anyway."

I wasn't sure what he meant by that. Maybe that we'd make a more permanent fence later? A chain-link fence, maybe. That would be stronger.

"I'll help when I'm not at school." Then I said, in a quieter voice, "I don't know if I could've shot him, Dad."

Dad didn't say anything for a while. When he finally answered, his voice sounded tired, and old. "I don't know if I could have, either, Paul. My folks raised me to take care of God's creatures. Not to hurt them. Not to kill them."

"Even the giant, black, ugly ones with tusks two feet long?"

"Well…I'm not absolutely sure about that." He put his arm over my shoulder, and he probably could tell I was still shaking a little. Which was crazy. The pig was gone. The birds and my dad and I were safe.

"I don't think he's coming back tonight," Dad said. "We can go back to bed."

When I'd crawled back under my green and white Hawaiian quilt that Auntie Sylvana made me, I could hear Dad and Mom talking in low voices so they wouldn't wake up Emily. I could hardly wait to tell my sister about the pig in the morning. She'd really be impressed! And Sal would want to hear every detail of the story. Tomorrow I'd enjoy the whole thing.

THREE

I really think I dream stuff every second that I'm asleep, I just forget most of it. Especially the scary dreams. I don't usually wake up screaming, like Sal did once when he was sleeping over. He woke up everybody in the house, he was yelling so loud. But sometimes I have to wake myself up to tell my mind what's real and what's a nightmare. This morning, that's what I had to do.

When I think about it now, I wonder why I didn't dream about the boar from last night. I would never admit it to Sal or Emmie, or probably even to my mom, but that thing scared the spit outta me. But while I was sleeping, there was no wild boar. Instead, somebody had ahold of both my arms, and I couldn't scream because there was something in my mouth.

Two big guys were dragging me along on the dirt, and another guy was in the back of Ray Salvador's beat-up old VW van. "Hurry up!" he yelled at them, and he opened the doors wider. "Get that little brat in here." When we were close enough, he laughed and helped the other guys pull me up and throw me on the floor of the van. I was face down and I smelled that thin, moldy rug Ray'd put back in there and felt little rocks on my cheek, and I knew that, some way or other, I had to wake up.

And when I finally did, I was hot and sweaty and I was taking big gulps of air, just like I was suffocating because of what was in my mouth in the dream. A gag, I guess it was. A rag that smelled like motor oil, mixed in with the mold smells and the being-afraid smells.

I don't know who the guys dragging me were, but the other guy was Raymond Salvador, Sal's big brother.

Raymond Jesus Salvador. You don't say his middle name like the Jesus in the Bible, Sal told me. You say it kinda like "Hey-zoos." But nobody ever said his whole name anyway. And if Sal wasn't an angel, like his name said, Ray sure as heck wasn't anything like the real Jesus. He was nineteen, way older than Sal, and for his whole life he'd had what my parents called "behavioral problems." That was a nice way of saying that Ray was a little bit crazy, but mostly just plain *mean.*

I didn't think I was afraid of Ray, really. He'd never done anything too mean to me, and that was the first dream I'd ever had about him. Most of the time he just ignored me. And when he didn't, he usually just kidded around with me and poked me like you would a little puppy, playing.

When I was a little kid, sometimes Ray'd get me laughing so hard from getting tickled, I'd be crying and not able to breathe and I'd start to panic, but I couldn't get up off Sal's bedroom floor because he was sitting on top of me. And I think I have some memories of Ray really hurting Sal and me when we were little, but they probably aren't real. It's hard to remember things right from small-kid-time.

Anyway, that was just how Ray was. He thought Sal and me were big wusses. He even gave us nicknames. Sissy Sallie for Sal was bad enough, but Ray especially liked what he came up with for me: Pansy Paulie. Man, I *really* loved that! I was just glad that most of the time we were there at his house when he used my nickname, so nobody else heard it.

And I can tell you this, too. Sal and me are not wusses. We're not babies. Ray just grins and laughs when we tell him that, though.

But in the dream, Ray was more like the Devil, and I really panicked before I could get myself awake all the way and get myself out of that stinking van and back into my own bed in my own bedroom.

Anyway, not a good way to wake up on a Sunday, all sweaty and shaky. But then I remembered the real-life excitement from last night, and I got up and washed and splashed water on my hair to kinda glue down the parts that were poking up. I got dressed and went in to wake up Emily. I just had to tell her about the pig before she heard about it from Mom or Dad. She was going to be really impressed!

Emily's six. There are almost as many years between us as there are between Raymond and Sal. But that's about the only thing that's the same with Ray and Emmie, because she's never been a behavioral problem kid. She's a girl—and a sister—so sometimes she's a pain. But that's mainly when she likes me too much and wants to be everywhere I am all the time. Or tells one of her stupid jokes. Even then, she's so cute I hardly ever get mad at her.

I went in Emmie's room and bounced on her bed until

she was awake enough to say, "Whaaat? Stop that, Paulie. Get off!" Then I told her the whole story, hardly exaggerating anything, and I was right—by the time I finished, she was sitting straight up and her brown eyes looked really big.

"Tell me again, Paulie. How did he *smell?*"

"The pig? It was about the awfulest smell I ever smelled. Like maybe he was shedding his hair and some skin, and the rotten pieces were all still hanging on there, stuck on him in big, stinky clumps. Or like...you remember that huge vulture when Uncle Porky took us to the Olomalu Zoo?"

"That ugly, gross bird? Sitting on his own little cement mountain in the cage? And the mountain was all slimy and white with vulture...you-know-what?"

"That's it. And the vulture had a half-eaten, rotten mongoose or something in his claws. Like that. The boar smelled like that except a hundred times worse."

"Ooooh! And how big was he, really?"

So of course I told her the truth about that, too, and she flopped back over on her pillow and pulled her blanket up to her neck. "That's so awesome, Paulie!"

And it was.

When Dad made us stop yakking and hurry up and have breakfast because we'd be late for Mass, I knew Emmie was still thinking about my pig. And even when we were down on our knees on the kneeler at St. Ann's Church, she whispered, "Will it come back tonight? I want to see him."

"Nope," I whispered back. "I scared him off with the rifle."

"Cool!"

FOUR

I had to wait until after church to tell Sal about the pig. Usually he's at St. Ann's with his mom and dad, but today his parents left really early in the morning to go back to the church retreat, so they let Sal sleep in. After church I walked over to his house and told him all about the boar. And he was just as excited as Emmie was, and he asked just about as many questions.

But I didn't say anything about dreaming about his brother. Which was kind of strange because me and Sal, we talk about everything. Even personal stuff. But we just talked about the boar and our science project. I even forgot about Raymond and the dream after a while.

But then, when we were in Sal's kitchen eating peanut butter and banana sandwiches, we heard Ray's van coming up the driveway.

The van door screeched open and in a minute, the front screen door slammed.

"I thought you said he wouldn't get home from Waiele until tonight!" I whispered.

Sal made an I-don't-know kind of face, then he said, "Something must've happened."

Something *had* happened, and Ray wasn't happy about it. "So," he said when he saw us there eating lunch, "da babies are home."

We mumbled, "Uh-huh." The peanut butter made it hard to say anything more or we'd have told him that we weren't babies.

"Well, good you here," Ray said, and we looked at him to see if he meant it. "Help wid da cages. I get five cages an some stuff in da van. You guys come help. Even fat, lazy little kids need to work."

Sal managed to ask, "Can we finish our sandwiches?" but we knew from the way Ray's eyes closed halfway that we'd probably never get to eat our lunch.

"Now!" was the only thing Ray said, and we scrambled out of our chairs and followed him out of the kitchen and over to the van where we heard some soft chicken noises inside.

When we were helping with the cages, Ray finally let us know why he came home early from Waiele. He was swearing and muttering to himself in pidgin—which his mom and dad hated just like mine did, but which he used all the time anyway—and going on and on about the cockfight.

By then we could have guessed what happened. Two of the five cages Ray handed down were empty. Another one had a big gray cock inside who looked okay, but he lurched to one side when he got up and tried to walk around in his cage. There wasn't any blood in there, but something was wrong with him.

I felt like throwing up when I looked inside the other two cages. A big Red was sitting in a pool of blood that was even redder than the feathers in his hackle, and the other guy, another Red, but a smaller one, seemed just as hurt as he was.

I looked at Sal, who'd put the smaller Red's cage down on the dirt and was staring inside it. His face turned white, then sad, and then really, *really* mad.

"You said you'd wait before you tested him!" Sal said, pointing at the Red. He looked like he was feeling just as sick as I was. "You told me to feed him only the best feed. Take care of him. He can be for show, for prizes. No gaffs, you said. No fighting. Maybe testing him with another rooster with gloves on, but no gaffs!" He stopped to get his breath and look away from the Red and over at his brother. He stood up and held the cage in front of Ray. "Look at him, Ray!"

Ray glanced down at the cage and swore. Then he said, "Yeah. I'm really pissed about dat one. Probably shoulda wrung his neck like dose two." He pointed to the empty cages. "I loss tree hunnerd bucks on dose losers. Ova tree hunnerd before dis one lose heart. Quit. Jus quit fighting. Turn aroun and walk away! How you tink I felt about dat, uh?"

Sal didn't answer at first. Then he opened the door on the top of the cage and started stroking his bird's feathers. "Red has heart. Plenty of heart! He just wasn't ready. Wasn't big enough. You said—"

"Oh, God!" Ray glared at Sal. "I shoulda left him dere. I knew it. Shoulda known you'd go all Bambi on me. Well, get it da hell outta here. I learn some lessons from him, at lease. One: Neva let Dad do da culling. Dis bird was alway skitzy. Showed you his okole wheneva you around him. Shoulda been culled out before we waste all dat time and feed and medicine on it. An numba two lesson. Not enough I have one terrible day. Shoulda known I'd have my baby brother blaming me cause his stupid bird lost. Git him da hell outta here."

"Where?" Sal squeaked.

I grabbed Sal's arm and looked up at Ray. "I'll take him home, okay? Me and Sal. We'll see what Uncle Porky can do with him."

"Sheesh!" Ray said. He was rubbing his long hair. "Two Bambi lovers. Sissie an Pansy. Two wusses. I get nuff problem wid jus one." He looked up, like to heaven, and then he finally said, "Go ahead den. Porky can take one look. An da big Red, too, an da Gray. Take um. Dey no good to me. Loosas. Keep um. Don't let me see um again or I'll finish um off."

Ray jumped down and a whiff of the van hit me in the face before he closed the doors. Just like the smells in my dream. The rug that I got thrown down on, and worse. Flattish, metal kinds of smells. Blood. I hate that smell. I ran around to the front of the van and leaned against its flat front until I could get enough breaths of air to get the smells out of my nose.

"Go back da house and finish clean up da sandwich mess now," Ray said—to Sal, I guess, because I don't think he could see me in front of the van, trying to keep from barfing.

But Sal told Ray no. Then he came around and handed one of the cages to me. He went back and brought the other two and we headed down his driveway on our way to my house. I saw some tears when I looked over at him, but right then I knew for sure that he was not a sissy. Sal Salvador was the bravest kid I knew.

FIVE

When we walked up my driveway, we saw a big flatbed truck parked by the infirmary and two guys carting fence stakes and wire mesh down to the far corner of the rooster yard. I couldn't believe my dad had already gotten somebody to come and start the fence. And on a Sunday, even. Then I saw it was his friends Manny and Bob, who always needed the work, so it made sense.

Dad was there giving the guys directions for where to put the stuff. When he saw us, though, he cut across and met us by the infirmary door. He looked inside the cage I was carrying, but he didn't say anything. Sal held out one of his cages, and Dad took it inside the infirmary and carried it over to the long table that runs across the middle of the room. Sal and me brought in the other cages.

Dad pulled on his gloves and handed a pair to Sal. He opened up the Gray's cage first, and Sal helped him take the rooster out and put him on the table. Dad felt under his wings and all along his neck and legs. "This one'll be okay, Sal. He's not hurt. Just a little leg problem, maybe. They must've decided not to fight him today."

"But he was walking funny, Dad," I said while the Gray was being put back in his travel cage.

"My guess is, he had a bad reaction to the stuff they doped him up with to make him anxious to fight. He probably started falling down and they realized they couldn't fight him."

Sal had already unclamped the little Red's cage door. His rooster wasn't still bleeding, but he was just lying there. "He can't even stand up," Sal whispered.

Dad made a whistling sound, like, "Wheww..." and turned to me. "Call your uncle, Paul. I don't think there's much hope for this one. How come your dad let him fight?" he asked Sal. "He's not old enough or strong enough for a derby."

All I heard when I went out of the infirmary door was Sal saying, "Ray took him to Waiele. He promised me he wouldn't fight him but..."

I hurried up to the house. Mom was washing lunch dishes when I went in the kitchen. "Hi, hon," she said. "What are you and Sal up to today?" She turned her head and looked at me. "Oh dear. What's happened, Paulie?"

"I have to call Uncle Porky." I was already dialing.

My auntie picked up right away and called Porky. It seemed like an hour before I heard him say, "Yeah, kid. What can I do you for?" just like always.

I explained, and my mom listened, so I didn't have to repeat everything after I hung up. Porky said he'd be over just as soon as he could get into his old clothes, and he must have changed really fast because his big truck pulled up by the infirmary in about three minutes. He took one look at the big Red and shook his head. "Too late for this one," he told Sal. "Lost too much blood too many hours ago."

My dad nodded. He'd known, I think, but he wanted us to hear it from Porky. He showed Porky Sal's bird, which looked just as bad as the big rooster to me. They examined him on the table, both of them talking real soft to the bird while they checked him out. Finally Porky looked at Sal. "I'll do what I can for him, Sal. Can't promise too much, but maybe he won't have to be put to sleep."

Sal leaned on the table. It looked like he was trying to catch his breath. Then he straightened up, really tall, and said, "Thanks, Mr. Silva."

"You can thank me later if your rooster pulls through," Uncle Porky said.

"Can I help you with him?" Sal asked.

Porky was carrying the bird to the operating table by then, but he'd seen Sal's face, I guess, because he said, "Better you two just hang out. Go somewhere. Do something to get your minds off all this." To my dad he said, "What's with the Gray?"

"Just drugs, I think. It's okay. Sal, you can take the Gray back home later, if you want to. Maybe wait a while for the stuff to wear off. Drugging the birds makes them want to fight harder, but it speeds up everything. Heart rate, blood pressure. This one just needs some rest—to come down after being so hyper. You guys can come back later and check on him if you want. Do what Porky said now, okay?"

Sal followed me and as we headed outside, we almost ran

into my mom. Her face didn't look happy or sad. Just kind of tired, the way she always looks when she thinks about the cockfighting. She puts up with it, but she's like Honey. It bothers her, I think.

She held out a plate of *malassadas.* "You had lunch?"

"Sort of. We were having sandwiches when Raymond got home. We didn't finish, though."

"Then you must be starving."

I looked at the plate of puffy round Portuguese doughnuts, all sugary outside, and for the first time in my life I said "No thanks" to my mom's malassadas. "I'm not too hungry. Sal?"

"Uh, not right now. Thanks anyway, Mrs. Silva."

"Okay. Porky must not have needed your help, so why don't you two go for a swim or something? I'll leave this plate inside for the other men."

I opened the infirmary door for her and I felt like stopping her and giving her a hug. I wasn't a man. I was her little kid. A hug would have felt really good right then, but I knew I had to get Sal away from there. So I closed the door and put my hand on Sal's shoulder and kind of steered him up to the house.

We sprawled out on the soft living room sofa. Sal hung over one end and I took the other side, one leg over the sofa's round arm. Milo gave my hand a whiskery, wet sniff, then he took off for the kitchen.

It took us a while to decide what to do with the rest of the afternoon, but we both knew Mom and everybody were right. We had to get out of there. But we didn't want to swim in the pond or play computer games or do any work on our science project. And we sure as heck didn't want to go over to Sal's and hang out with Raymond!

"That movie, *The Last Samurai.* It's back now at the Ilima Theater, Sal. It's supposed to be good and I never saw it when it came out a long time ago. Wanna go?"

"Um…yeah, but not today, I think."

"Wanna fish off the bridge? I've got an extra bamboo, so you wouldn't have to go home and get your pole."

"Guess I'm not in the mood right now."

"Then what? You got any ideas?"

"I was just thinking. You know my Grampa Salvador?"

"Sure. I met him three or four times, maybe. At your house, and at the baby luau for your cousin at that Chinese restaurant. The one with the really good noodles. He seems like a neat old guy."

"I never took you over to his house, though, right?"

"Nope. I woulda remembered."

"Maybe we should go there now. The bus'll be coming up the hill pretty soon." He looked at his watch. "We've got about fifteen minutes. We could catch it. My mom should be back home by now so I'll call her. You see if you can go with me."

My mom said it was okay, just to be back in time for supper. Sal phoned home, and it was okay with his mom, too, and then he checked with his grampa who must have said, sure, come on over.

Sal and me took turns in the bathroom. I splashed water on my hair and smoothed it down, but it didn't help much.

Then we walked to the road where the jitney bus, this little bus with a roof but no windows, picked us up. It was a good idea, going down to see Sal's grampa. He might be able to cheer Sal up.

SIX

When we were riding down the hill, hitting every bump in the road, Sal looked over at me with a little grin on his face. "My grampa asked who you were. 'He da Silva kid? The Portagee one wit da hair?'"

"What did he mean by that?"

"Paulie. Don't you *ever* look at your hair? It's always *kapakahi.* It goes in every direction."

"Hey. I comb it. I just have a bunch of cowlicks, that's all." I pointed to the hair sticking up on the back of my head. When Mr. Mitsuda, our barber, sees it, he always says he has no idea how he can cut around all the *giri-giris*—that's the Japanese word for cowlicks, I think.

"This giri-giri's the worst," I told Sal. "It's like a whirlpool kind of thing, and it makes my hair go whichever way it wants to. Look, there's another one here, and here—"

Sal laughed. "So that's what my grampa meant. That's how he remembers people. The one with the hair. The one that all-time is eating. The one with the mouth—that's my Auntie Consuelo, who talks a mile a minute. He's not making fun.

It's just how he remembers people. He's getting pretty old. He forgets names."

"How old is he?"

"I'm not sure. Eighty-three. Maybe eighty-four. He's finally starting to slow down a little. Has arthritis pains from all of the years he worked the sugarcane after he moved here from the Philippines."

"Where in the Philippines? Manila?" Manila was the only place in the Philippines I knew the name of.

Sal shook his head. "Nope. His family lived in Laoag, in Ilocos Norte. My dad said Grampa was fifteen when he came here with a big bunch of workers. Most were young, like him. They worked really hard digging, planting, weeding, cutting sugarcane every day."

"They got paid, didn't they?"

"Yeah, but hardly anything. They did have little houses and could buy stuff at the plantation store. And have a little money left over to send back home."

"Doesn't sound like much fun for somebody who's only fifteen."

"You had to be super strong for that kind of thing, Paulie. I mean, *super* strong. Grampa said you had to use your machete to hack through the tough cane, and you had to work in the hot sun until it was dark. The *lunas*, the bosses, worked those guys like slaves."

I started thinking about my dad's family, who came from Madeira and the Azores to work on the plantations. "The Portuguese who came. Do you know anything about them?"

"About the same. Some got to be lunas, but most just worked the cane like my grampa. They came over later, I think. Anyways, there were different camps for the Chinese and Filipinos and Portagees and Japanese. You can ask my grampa if you want. He has plenty of stories."

After about fifteen minutes, we jumped down off the bus by the dirt road Sal said his grampa lived on. I could hear roosters crowing somewhere down the road. Some scraggly patches of old abandoned sugarcane grew high on either side of it, their dried-up roots sticking out of reddish dust. We kicked up lots of the dust when we walked to a bunch of little cottages. Maybe eight or nine of them. Some looked empty. Some looked like somebody lived there, but they never bothered to paint or weed or anything. But the little house Sal pointed to, at the end of the row, was nice and neat. It had nice clean paint. A dark greenish blue color, with the window frames white.

The tiny yard in front had a couple of hibiscus bushes with bright red flowers and some anthuriums in a row by the road. I saw three roosters walking along in front of the house. I'd heard crowing when we got off the bus, and I thought these were the roosters who'd been making the noise. Then I looked again and said, "Hey…what the heck?" and I heard Sal laugh.

"They're plastic, Paulie. My grampa is a real old-time cocker. He *loves* his birds. You'll see."

"I like his house."

"You're gonna like him, too. He's cool. And he remembered you."

"Yeah. 'The one with the hair.'"

Sal called out "Hello?" while he pulled the screen door open for me.

An old-sounding voice answered him. "Back here, Sal. Come back da kitchen. Get some *lumpia* fo you. Jus make. Da grampa's one good cook, I tell you. Come."

Sal headed straight for the kitchen in back, but I had to stop and look around.

Man! The whole living room was one big rooster place! Not real ones, of course, but every kind of rooster you've seen in your life. A rooster quilt and about ten pillows were on the worn-out green sofa. All the pillows had different kinds of birds on them. A gigantic oil painting of a rooster I didn't recognize hung on the wall above the sofa, and little rooster pictures were on all the other walls. Roosters, roosters, and more roosters. Some were photographs of birds standing in sunlight, getting stroked by somebody who must have been Grampa Salvador when he was younger.

An old-looking cupboard had at least a dozen shelves filled with—you guessed it—roosters. Every color, every size. Plastic, china, bobble-head roosters. Wooden puppet roosters. Pairs fighting and pairs challenging each other to see who was the biggest, the most beautiful. Shiny rooster trophies on some of the shelves.

Sal wasn't kidding. His Grampa Salvador sure was one old cocker!

I backed up until I could see the whole case. Up on top of it there were five life-sized roosters. Stuffed, of course. I knew they weren't alive from the minute I saw them. But the middle guy was staring right down at me. He gave me the creeps.

So did a little glass case that was full of gaffs, the curved, razor-sharp spurs that they fasten to the fighting cocks' legs. There were maybe twenty gaffs in there, all shiny, like Grampa had just polished them. I'd never liked gaffs, so I turned around and gave the rest of the room a quick once-over, then I headed for the kitchen.

Sal was munching on a crispy, deep-fried lumpia. He'd already launched into pidgin, which, I found out in a minute was the only language his grampa talked.

"You favorite, Paul," Sal said, chewing away. "Shrimp, pork in deese. Here. Dis Paul, Grampa. You rememba Paul."

The dark, wrinkled little man winked at me. "Silva, no?" he said. "One beeg-mout Portagee?"

"Yup," I said, smiling at the insult. "That's me."

"Portagee and *haole*, Grampa," Sal said. "Pull haole from da mudda side." He was right—my dad was Portuguese and my mother was haole—white, Caucasian. "Da fadda's Robert Silva," he added.

"Course I know Robert. You get good family, little Silva. Da fadda one good breeda. He one okay-kine guy."

"Thanks, Mr. Salvador. I'll tell him you said that."

"Can call me Alberto, Paulie," he said, pushing the plate more in front of me. "Hey, Sal, don't eat um all, huh? Geev to da fren, kay?"

And after a while, I was as stuffed with the Filipino spring rolls as the roosters on the cabinet were stuffed with…well, stuffing. Sal and his grampa and me sat around the kitchen table and finished up the whole platter, dipping them in a bowl of warm, great-tasting, salty-sweet sauce, dripping the sauce on the old yellow tablecloth. The yellow oilcloth that had bright red roosters marching around on its edges.

* * *

Finally Sal wiped his chin with his napkin and told his grampa, "Paulie like know bout ole days in da Philippines, kay? An bout da roostas?"

Grampa Salvador looked across the table at me, his eyes crinkling at their corners. "You like, Paul?"

I wondered if he meant did I want to hear, or did I just like roosters. So I just said "Sure" to both.

Mr. Salvador—Alberto—leaned his head back, remembering. "Was six den. Maybe seven. Da fadda take me see his bes roosta first fight. Was prize winna already, dat bird, an was da first fight. But da fadda, he know. An he know I need see um. Can neva forget."

His story was a long one. His dad's little rooster faced a huge, strong bird that had won a lot of derbies. It was like David and Goliath, he said, and when it ended, David won and everybody cheered like mad and Alberto's whole family got congratulated. Everybody wanted to buy the winner, but "Da fadda neva sell. Neva. Da roosta, he get *heart.* Ahhh, dance, dat bird! Wid da beeg Gray, like one ballet dance."

Alberto stopped and laughed at the imaginary picture he was painting for us. "Nah, nah. Ballet too fancy. But da birds dance, move like music, use wing, curve neck. Dance, dance."

He waved his hands, one with fingers spread out like feathers on the birds' wings, the other curved like a long, twisting neck.

"Was small-kid-time den," he said as he finished his story, "but ole Alberto neva forget."

"Heart, Grampa? Da bird get plenny heart?"

"Like no bird eva I see my whole life!" He turned to me and grabbed my wrist. I knew this was something important to him. "Jus watch um, Paulie, watch one bird like dat, you get heart, too. Get strong. Get beautiful, like da roosta."

I nodded. I was glad we'd come. I'd never thought much about the fights, and never in the way that the old man talked about them. He told us maybe a dozen more stories about when he was young, and in every one of them, a rooster was the hero. A rooster with heart. In one, the bird cut Alberto's hand with the gaff when he saw his opponent, he was so anxious to get down to business. "Scramble right outta da hans, Paulie. Was born fo fight, see. Was breed fo fight, an das all."

Sal and I listened to his grampa without saying anything. We didn't want to break the spell, didn't want to bring the old man back to life here, today, where he had to walk slow, had to be happy just to have a few roosters in his backyard and fake roosters everywhere else.

Finally Alberto stood up and got himself a glass of water. "Da mout dry, das why. Too much talk!" Sal looked at his watch then and said we'd better head out for home. Alberto put his glass on the table and went over to his little refrigerator. He pulled out a plastic bowl of something—Sal told me its name but I forget—some sort of Filipino pudding, and he handed it to Sal. "Geev da mudda, Sal. Good kine."

"You make, Grampa?"

He winked at me. "Course I make! Da grampa, he one good cook, uh? One chef. Tell da mudda geev you one lil tase, den eat res tonight. Keep cole, uh? In icebox til can eat."

"Tanks, Grampa," Sal said, taking the bowl.

As we walked out of the kitchen, I thanked him, too. "Tanks, uh? Fo lumpia. Stories."

Alberto shook his head. "Nah, nah," he said as we crossed the living room. He must have seen me looking at the painting of the really big rooster hanging over the sofa because he added, "Hey, Paulie. Nice, uh? Nex time, I tell bout dat guy, kay?"

"Great. Neva saw one roosta like dat, Alberto."

"Not in Hawaii, I tink. Was one Sweater Yellow-legged Hatch. One thoroughbred, champion of da Philippines. Of da world."

"Wow. So, nex time. We'll be back. Right, Sal?"

"I bring Paulie, Grampa, kay?"

"Sure, sure. Come. Mos time da grampa home now."

Sal stopped before he opened the screen door and turned around. "So, Grampa...bring Ray, too?"

Alberto's eyes squinted at Sal, and really quick, Sal said, "Jus kidding, uh...but Ray comes see you, uh? Comes sometimes?"

The old man folded his arms over his chest and slumped down into his chair. "Wen need money. Das wen." The smile he'd had when he told his stories was gone. He took a deep breath and then let it out in a long, slow whistle. "Problem, dat kid. All time problem. Say prayer for dat one." He looked up at Sal, then over at me, then he said, "Da roostas, jus fo money. Ray like money…Raymond like blood."

Sal nodded. "He no like me, no like Paulie, for sure."

Alberto frowned. "You an Paul too gooda frens, I tink. So Ray no like. Make him feel bad. Jealous."

"But Ray has frens, Grampa."

"Get frens, yes. Dat Tafasau kid. Da big, mean one."

"Roger."

"Yeah, an Kenny Aguilar." Grampa Alberto shook his head. "Jus like Ray, dat. An still hang aroun wit Keanu, wat da name? Perreira, yeah? Right. Frens. Ha! Not frens. Jus gang. Try stay away dose guys, if can. No love. No love nobody, dat Raymond. Why? Dunno. Lotta hate."

He rested his elbows on his skinny knees and his chin on his hands. He was quiet for a minute, but then he looked back and forth at Sal and me. "I tink," he said to Sal, "if Raymond could, he make you fight, you and Paulie. Put gaff on legs. Tie sharp beak on face, watch, watch da fight. Wait fo blood. Fo you to hate da udda one, too, like him. You too gooda frens fo Ray. I say prayer. Too much hate, dat boy."

He pushed himself up from the chair, and I shook my head fast, trying to get the picture of Sal and me fighting in a cockpit out of my mind. That was all I needed, something else to give me nightmares!

"Well!" Alberto said then, the smile coming back. "Ansa you question, Sal? No bring da brudda dis house, kay? Til

Ray no mo hate. But you come, kay? See da grampa anytime. An da Portagee. He come."

Sal said we'd be back soon, and we went out the screen door into the sunny front yard. We walked past the plastic roosters, then we turned around and waved to Alberto. Sal held up the white plastic Save-A-Lot bag holding the container of pudding. "Mahalo, Grampa. See ya."

As we walked back down the dusty road I told Sal, "About your grampa. I like him. He's one old cocker, all right! He's one really cool old guy."

SEVEN

The jitney that took us back up the hill came late, and when I finally got back home, I got *the look* from Mom. She and Dad and Emily were already having dinner.

"Well, Mr. Silva," my dad said to me. "We thought you'd be home half an hour ago."

He didn't sound really mad, so quick, I rinsed off my hands in the kitchen sink and plunked down in my chair. I told him what Sal and I had been doing, including Alberto's compliment. "He said you were a good man, Dad. A good breeder, too."

"That's high praise from Mr. Salvador. Roosters are that old man's life."

"You don't have to tell me that. You should see his house!" I told about some of the rooster stuff.

"Cool," Emily said. "Maybe I can come with you guys sometime to visit Mr. Salvador."

"He lets me call him Alberto. Yeah, maybe sometime, if Sal wants."

I dug into my dinner. I wasn't really starving because of all the lumpia, but my mom's *vinha doce* tasted great anyway. I had to talk between bites. Except for Portuguese sweet bread and malassadas, it's my favorite Portuguese food she makes. She pickles the pork pieces in salt water and vinegar and spices for a long time, then she cooks them with this thick, vinegary sauce to go on your rice.

Emily was busy eating, too, but when I finished the David and Goliath and the rooster ballet stories, she looked at me kinda strange.

"Mr. Salvador likes the fighting, too?" she asked.

"He likes anything that has to do with roosters. Including the fights."

"Well, I don't," she said. "Making them fight is cruel. I'll never go to a fight, that's for sure."

"Not even if I get Raymond to take you?"

Everybody stopped eating then and stared at me. "Just kidding!" I said. "You know I was kidding, Emmie, right?"

"Well, that's not a nice thing to kid about," she said, sticking her chin out and frowning at me. "Not funny, Paul. Not funny *at all.*"

* * *

Mondays aren't too bad. They're mostly good for me, because I don't hate school. My mom scouted out all the schools around here when we moved and found one she thought was better than even the Catholic schools, and that's how Emmie and me ended up at Kaukani School. It's not a church school, but it's a good private school. Anyway, there aren't any bullies at Kaukani that I know of—nobody to say they'd pound your ugly face if they see you again on Monday or something. That's better than some of the public schools in Hawaii. Some of them have real problems.

When I woke up on Monday, I thought about all the crazy things that had gone on over the weekend. The stuff about Ray still bothered me when I thought about it, and so did the stuff about Sal's poor rooster, even though Dad said he was recuperating and would probably get well. I decided it was going to be good to get back to school and get a break from real life.

The school bus doesn't come this far up the mountain, so Mom and Mrs. Salvador usually take turns getting us to school. We have a station wagon and Sal's dad bought a nice SUV after he got a promotion at the hotel where he works, so there's plenty of room for carpooling.

Just last week, Dad started driving again. He was really stoked, because it took tons of therapy to be able to do that. Before, we'd drop him off at the rehab center on Alakine Street on our way to school. It's pretty modern and it has all kinds of cool stuff, especially the big pool they use for water therapy. The first time I saw it I wanted to swim there, but Dad said I'd have to get injured or sick first, so I'm sticking with the swimming hole Sal and I have up above our houses.

The first kid I saw after I lugged my books into Mrs. Chong's homeroom on Monday was Honey. I dumped my backpack on the floor by my desk. Then, real cool, I said, "Howzit?"

"Fine," she said.

I couldn't think of anything else to say, so I just fished around in my bag for my math book. While we weren't talking I took a quick look at her, though. She had a kinda pinkish plumeria in her hair, and it matched her pink tank top. Her tan looked nice, but I couldn't say that so finally I asked, "How was fishing with your dad?"

She looked over at me. "Fine. We went yesterday, too. Dad had some extra time. I think he's trying to spend more time doing stuff together. It's nice."

"Yeah. My dad's trying that, too. Of course, it's easier because he doesn't have to go to the lumberyard. Just works at home now."

"Uh-huh. Anyway, I told my dad about your place, and the roosters and everything. Told him it was nice. Mahalo for showing me around. It was interesting, Paulie. Nice."

"Yeah? You can come back if you want to sometime. No problem."

"Okay. Sure."

Sal came in then and interrupted our great conversation. He looked at Honey and said, "Heard you guys had a date on Saturday."

Honey glared at him. "Hey...*not!* No date! Paul just showed me around his place, that's all." Then she looked at Sal's grin and must have seen that he was just trying to bug her so she calmed down and said, "You're a total pain, *Angel* Salvador. I'm never going up to *your* farm, that's for sure."

"Hey. Who invited you anyways?"

I liked it when Honey and Sal gave each other a bad time. I guess that was because I didn't feel like teasing Honey, so when they went at it, it made Honey seem more…more like one of the guys, I guess. Just the way she's been since kindergarten.

I went out to the restroom while they were talking. Looked around the hall on the way. Yup. Everything was normal again. The custodian had polished the green and black linoleum floors so slick you almost had to skate your way over to the restroom. Even in your worn-out rubber sandals—we just call the flip-flops "slippas"—you could skid. Kids were coming in and high-fiving each other, or just flashing shaka signs or yelling at each other. Mrs. Murakami, our principal, stuck her face out of her office door and told a couple of kids to pipe down.

I almost ran smack into my friend Junior Reeves, who was shoving his way into the restroom. "Howzit, brah?" he asked and thumped me on the back. "Do anyting ova da weeken?"

"Nah," I said. When we'd finished peeing, I told him, "Well—get one wild peeg try eat da roostas. Was kinda fun."

"Cool! One beeg bugga?"

"One *monsta*, man! Gotta build one fence now."

Junior seemed impressed. "You kill da bugga?" he asked as he gave his hands a quick rinse in the long sink.

"Nah. Scare um away wid da rifle."

We were out the door before Junior answered, "Ah. Too bad, uh? My fren's auntie make da bes Portagee sausage, das why. Delicious. So *ono!*"

"Bet my mom's sausage mo betta."

"Really? Invite me ova, den, kay?"

"Sure. So, nex time. See ya."

We headed for our rooms. Junior has Mr. Armstrong—the only man teacher at Kaukani—for homeroom and first period. I dived into my seat right when the bell rang. Sal nodded at me and whispered, "Good timing, man." Then Mrs. Chong, who had her short black hair in a new hairdo but still looked just like Mrs. Chong, glanced around the room. She can take roll in about five seconds without even calling our names.

After a while, she pulled a couple of chairs over to her desk and called us up two at a time for conferences about our science fair projects. I watched Honey and her friend Amy sit down in the two chairs, and while Sal and I waited, I thought about what it would be like to be partners with Honey.

"Hey!" I heard Sal say, and my pictures of Honey and me at the library, and then Honey and me using my computer together at my house, disappeared. "Didn't you hear her call us?" He grabbed my arm and steered me to one of the chairs in front.

"Well, gentlemen," Mrs. Chong said. "Can I begin to guess what you'll be studying for your project?"

We answered at the same exact time: "Roosters." Then all three of us laughed.

"It looks like I *could* begin to guess, then, after all," Mrs. Chong said. "I probably should have resisted your plea to be partners in this, but I know you enjoy each other's company." She wrote something down with her big green pen and then looked up at us. "Well?" she said. "You know the routine. You need to tell me just what aspect of roosterdom you've decided to work on. It's not enough simply to have a subject. What is the problem you'll try to solve?"

We were ready for that. I told her we were planning to study the process of culling.

"Culling?" she asked.

"Yeah. Weeding out the birds that are too weak or not brave enough to survive."

"Survival, meaning just staying alive?" Mrs. Chong asked, looking at me.

"Not exactly. I mean..."

"Survival in the ring, Mrs. Chong," Sal said. "In the cock-pit. The birds have to have certain qualities or they won't make it through their first fight. We're going to study those."

"And just what happens to the birds that don't have those qualities, Mr. Salvador?"

"Well. Some of them don't even hatch. Other ones have to be put to sleep. For their own good. So we're going to study all of this."

Mrs. Chong looked at Sal, then at me. She propped her elbows on her desk and leaned her chin on her knuckles. That wasn't too easy, because Mrs. C. was really short and her desk was pretty high. She didn't say anything for a while.

Then she said, "No, gentlemen. You are not. You are not advancing science with a project that encourages cruelty at all levels. I know I asked you to study something that you knew about, a subject that interested you. But this one just won't do."

We both gave a little groan but didn't argue. What Mrs. Chong was doing wasn't fair, but she was the teacher and when teachers make up their minds, nobody can change them.

"So, Mr. Silva and Mr. Salvador, it's 'back to the old drawing board' for you. You still have time to come up with a project, but I want you to *think* about it. Even scientists need to have ethical values, you know. Some day you'll be happy that I didn't just say 'anything goes' on this project. Question things, gentlemen. Question, and you'll find answers that can shape your beliefs."

We nodded, but after we were back in our desks and two other guys were sitting up in the hot seats, Sal looked at me like he had no idea what was going on. And I don't think I had much more idea than he did. I was starting to get mad at Mrs. Chong. Why was everybody giving me a hard time about the roosters all of a sudden?

Sal looked up to make sure Mrs. C. wasn't watching us, then whispered, "'Back to the drawing board.' That's crazy, you know. There's nothing wrong with the culling. Bet they do that with the chickens we eat. What do you want to bet they cull out the little scrawny ones and don't breed them? Right?"

"Right," I said, and I didn't even whisper. "Man. What does she want from us, anyway?"

"She wants us to question? Well, I have a question for her," Sal said. He had his head forward on his neck, just like roosters do when they strut around. "I should've asked about the chickens and turkeys she'll be roasting for Mr. Chong's dinner. Just how did they get so big and fat, huh?"

"Right," I said again.

Sal let out his breath with a big puff. "It's just a woman's thing, Paulie. We can't let it get to us. So tonight I'll come over and we'll go back to that old drawing board."

"Jennifer Leinala said she and Hannah are working on plant DNA."

"No way! That stuff's invisible, you know. No—we'll work on roosters, okay? We'll just work on something that won't turn Mrs. Chong off this time."

"Maybe we could take her over to see your grampa, Sal. Bet he could talk her into any rooster project his favorite grandson wanted to do."

Sal thought that over. He must have had the same picture in his mind as I did, because he stopped frowning then and he got a kind of crooked smile on his face. It was funny, imagining Mrs. Chong in the rooster house, listening to Mr. Salvador's stories and eating lumpia with the sauce dripping down to her elbows. I wasn't mad at Mrs. C. anymore when I saw that picture in my head. We'd just have to find something to study that wouldn't bug her.

EIGHT

Sal walked over after dinner, but we never got back to the old drawing board. When he opened the front screen door he said, “This door always squeaks, Paul. You need to oil it or something.” Then he plunked down on our big green sofa and just looked at me kinda funny. Not happy or sad or even excited. Just this strange look.

“So what’s up?” I asked him. “You wanna do another computer search on the rooster thing?”

“Oh, yeah. The project. Not right now. I probably should go home in a while.”

“Go home? Sal, you just got here. What the heck’s going on?”

He chewed on his lower lip before he answered, and I knew something had happened. I sat down on the sofa by him and just waited.

“Well,” he said after a while. “Ray’s in jail.”

“In jail? Your brother’s in jail? What’s he doing there? Did they raid a cockfight—”

“No. It didn’t have anything to do with that. A couple of cops came to our house when we were almost ready to eat, and I answered the door. 'Does a Raymond Jesus Salvador live here?' one guy asked me, and I said yes, and he said, 'Is he home now?' and I guess I nodded. 'May we come in and talk with him, please?' All polite. So what could I do? I said come in and I'll get him, and they did, and I went back to Ray's room. He was sacked out on his bed, but he jumped up quick when I told him. He looked wide-awake when he passed by me in the hallway."

"Man," I said. "So did you listen in? When they talked to him, I mean?"

He shook his head. "My dad was talking with them by then. I was going to listen but my mom grabbed my arm and said, 'Let your father and Raymond take care of this, Sal. They probably just need some information from Ray.' But when we were back in the kitchen and she passed me my hamburger, her hand was shaking."

I wanted Sal to talk quicker and finish the story, but he looked kinda shaky then, too, so I kept quiet. He locked his fingers around the back of his neck and kept them there while he looked up, maybe at something on the ceiling.

Finally he said, "They arrested Ray for fighting, Paulie, not for cockfighting. Dad came in and got his car keys out of the basket in the kitchen. 'Ray's got himself in some kind of trouble,' he said. 'Something about a fight, him and Keanu and that Aguilar boy. I'm taking him down to the station. I'll tell you what's happened when we get back.'"

"But just your dad came home?" I asked.

"Yeah. He came home…I don't know how long he was gone. Mom had already put their plates in the fridge, so she took one out to heat up for Dad, but he said he wasn't hungry. He said that Ray and the Aguilar kid got pretty drunk last night, and so did these two guys at Kimo's Bar and Grill—that's where they always hang out. Dad told us that Ray said the other guys started in on Ray and them first. Calling them names, pushing, and then he and Kenny Aguilar and Roger Tafasau—Roger got there about then—pounded the hell out of the two of them."

"So mostly just the other guys got hurt?"

"Roger broke one guy's nose and cracked his rib, and the cops said he was lucky that was all, because Roger outweighed him by at least a hundred pounds. That guy'll be okay. But the other guy's at Kukui Memorial. He has a concussion from where Ray clubbed him on the head with a beer bottle."

"A beer bottle? Oh, man!"

Sal took a deep breath before he said, "My mom started crying and she said Raymond could never have done that and my dad held onto her. She looked over at me and I knew not even my mom believed that Ray wouldn't hit somebody if he was mad. And drinking. Dad said Ray told him the other guy started it and it was a fair fight."

"Maybe it was, Sal," I said. "Maybe Ray was telling the truth."

He shook his head. "Thanks. But you don't believe it either, do you?"

I didn't answer.

"Anyways, Dad got on the phone. He called his uncle Bert, the one who's a bail bondsman, to try to get Ray out of jail, but he couldn't, so maybe tomorrow Ray'll come home. So that's about it." Sal took another deep breath and let it come back out really slow.

I tried to think of something to say, but all I could think of was Roger Tafasau, who's as big and as mean as a bull, pounding some little guy, and Ray, who's pretty big himself for being pure Filipino, fighting the other guy with a beer bottle, and probably Kenny Aguilar getting in punches wherever he could.

I didn't like thinking about it so I said, "So you think Ray'll get out tomorrow?"

"Maybe. It depends on if Bert can get bail set and stuff. Dad said it also depends on what happens to the guy in the hospital, if his condition changes. And what charges they'll file. We'll probably know in the morning."

"Well," I heard myself saying, "I'm not sorry that Ray's in jail. I'd be happy if he had to stay there for a long, long time."

Then I saw Sal's face and I knew in a second I shouldn't have mouthed off.

Real quiet, he said, "I know that's how you feel, Paulie. Sometimes I feel that way about him, too. And I'm not saying he doesn't deserve some kind of punishment…but Ray's my brother. Can you understand that?"

"Yeah…I guess so." Then I said I was sorry, but I think I was more surprised than sorry—about Sal. I didn't really think until right then that Sal cared anything about his rotten brother. How could anybody care about Ray?

"Ray's my brother," Sal said again, and then he got up.

"Well, anyways. I just was going to tell you what happened, so I'd better get back home now. You know."

"Yeah. We don't have to work on the project tonight."

"My mom's pretty shook. Dad's okay, I think. Mostly mad at Ray. This isn't how he's raised his sons, he keeps saying, and that's true. So…laters, Paulie."

"Yeah. Laters."

I walked outside with him and he turned around like he was going to say something else, but then he just headed off down the driveway.

* * *

It was getting dark. The lights were on in the infirmary so I went inside. I was glad Uncle Porky wasn't there this time. Just Dad. He was scrubbing down a portable rooster cage. He stopped when he saw me and asked me what was up.

"Ray Salvador's in jail," I told him. "He hurt a guy pretty bad in a fight."

"Oh, no…somehow that doesn't surprise me, though. Was it just the two of them?"

"No. Ray and Roger Tafasau and Kenny Aguilar against two other guys, I don't know who they were."

"That figures. Three against two. Probably those three big guys against two little scrawny ones. That's how Ray operates. He's been in some pretty bad fights before, and never just one against one." He cleaned the cage a little more. "The roosters have a much better chance in their fights."

"Yeah," I said. "At least their fights are fair."

I hadn't thought of that before. Score one for the cockfights! I needed to remember that the next time somebody gave me a bad time about them.

"If Ray's in jail this time," Dad said, "it must have been bad."

"Sal says he clubbed this guy with a beer bottle at Kimo's."

Dad squeezed his eyes shut tight for a second. "Sounds like we're going to have to do some heavy-duty praying for the other guy, huh?" I nodded. Then he said, "And extra prayers for Raymond. He'll need them just as much."

"Ray?" I asked. I couldn't believe I'd heard him right. "Ray Salvador? He doesn't deserve any prayers. And he sure doesn't deserve his nice family! They don't deserve *him*, that's for sure. I'll pray for them, and for the guy in the hospital, but not for Ray."

Dad started back to work. He scraped a corner of the cage with a wire brush. Then he said, "I hope you'll change your mind about that. Pray for Ray, too, Paul. God made him and God loves him. Ray needs all the help he can get if he's ever going to turn his life around. Think about it, okay?"

I said okay, I'd think about it, then I went over to look at the chicks. One had just hatched, and he was having a hard time standing up. He was messy and ugly and not at all fuzzy and cute yet. I watched him finally stand up, and something made me remember what Dad said about the wild boar. About not harming one of God's creatures.

I couldn't help it then. I had to ask the question that had been bothering me ever since Honey said that looking at our beautiful roosters made her feel sad.

"Dad?"

"Yes?"

"If you believe we shouldn't hurt anybody else—even wild pigs and roosters and Raymond Salvador—well, then, how come we raise roosters who we know are going to get hurt? Or going to hurt somebody else?"

Dad didn't look at me. I thought he might be mad. But when he did answer finally, his voice wasn't mad.

"Son," he said, "I'm afraid that's a question you'll need to answer for yourself."

"But *why*, Dad?"

"You're growing up, Paul. You're going to have to figure out some things on your own."

That's all he said, so I watched him for a while. Then I grabbed a brush and another cage and went at it, getting it so clean even my mom would have approved.

When we were finished Dad said thanks for helping. For the rest of the night I kept thinking about what he'd said. I wonder if I'll ever figure out what he meant.

NINE

When you live on an island, you don't think much about everybody who doesn't live on one. You grow up in Hawaii and you get used to the way things are here. You know there are places that don't have ocean all around them. Places where you don't give directions to drive *mauka,* toward the mountains, or *makai,* toward the ocean. I was thinking about that when we drove makai to school the next morning.

It's a long way, maybe two miles. I guess most kids from the mainland would think that was short because maybe they ride a bus ten miles to school. And on vacations, they get loaded into their cars and drive hundreds of miles—sometimes even thousands—to vacation at places like lakes or national parks or Disneyland. Not us. We go twenty miles to the Olomalu Zoo and we think we made this really long trip.

It was Mom's turn to pick up Sal again, and he climbed into the backseat of the wagon with Emmie and me. I was hoping he'd know more about Ray, but when I asked, "Anything new?" he just shook his head. "Too early, I guess," I said. He didn't even look at me, so I got the hint. He just wanted to forget the whole thing.

But on an island like ours, that's impossible. When I was little, there was this radio guy who talked about how fast the news gets around in Hawaii. He called it "the Coconut Wireless." I didn't understand what he meant then, but I figured it out later. Here, if one person knows a secret, it gets to everybody else on your island in about ten seconds. You don't even have to e-mail or phone.

We were climbing out of the car by the school's front lawn when Kevin Pang ran over to Sal and grabbed his shoulder.

"Eh! Sallie. Ray stay jail?"

After that, everybody at Kaukani School started in on Sal. The Coconut Wireless was working, all right. Ray being arrested was probably on the Internet already.

Sal and me kept telling everybody, "We don't know what's going on," which was true, but they wanted more. By the time we got to Mrs. Chong's room, I could tell that Sal was almost ready to scream.

Honey was sitting there reading something and when she looked up, Sal said to her, "I don't know. Yes, he is. Yeah, I hope the other guy's okay. End of statement."

Honey stared at him like he'd worn Batman pajamas to school or something. "And good morning to you, too, Sal!" she said. She put her book down on her desk. "What the heck are you talking about?"

She hadn't heard! One person on this whole island hadn't heard about Ray's fight.

Sal said to me, "You might as well tell her," and then he left, so I did tell her—just the basic facts.

After, Honey said, "Poor Sal…and Sal's poor mom and dad."

"Yeah," I said. "And poor guy who got conked on the head with a beer bottle. That's who I feel sorry for."

She said, "Of course, Paulie," and I took off quick for my own desk. She might've asked me to pray for poor Raymond Salvador like my dad did, and I sure wasn't ready to do that.

* * *

I didn't hear anything more about Raymond all day, but right after we got home from school, Sal phoned me.

"The guy Ray hit's doing a little better," he said, almost whispering.

I guessed that Ray was back home. "That's good news."

"Yeah. He'll probably get out of Kukui Memorial tomorrow. He was over here from Honolulu. He must be a nice guy, because my mom told me that he's not pressing charges or anything."

"Wow! Ray must be happy about that."

Sal waited a minute before he answered me. I heard a door slam, hard. Then he said, "Believe me, he is *not* happy. Not happy *at all!* I'm getting out of here. Meet you at the pond."

"Five minutes," I said. I already had my shirt halfway off before I hung up the phone.

* * *

Sal was there before I was and I could tell he was ready to talk. He said Ray'd had another fight, this time with their dad. Ray hadn't hit him or anything, but they must've been fighting ever since his dad picked Ray up at the police station. They were still yelling at each other in the kitchen when Sal got dropped off after school.

"Mom was leaving when I got to the front porch," he said. "She told me about the guy getting better and asked if I wanted to go with her to get groceries. I said I'd stay outside 'til things calmed down, but I should've escaped with her."

We waded to the deep part of the pool. "Dad said he wished Ray'd had to stay in jail for a couple of months, like he deserved," Sal told me.

"So I'm not the only one who—"

Sal turned around and gave me a look, but he didn't defend his stupid brother. "Ray said it was all Dad's fault. Ray feels like he never gets treated like a man, and he told Dad he'd rather be in jail than live at home. He would've moved in with Roger a long time ago except for the roosters, because that's the only work he has now. Dad told him to go right ahead and move out.

"You should've heard them, Paulie. They were really going at it. 'You pull stuff like this and I wonder if you're really my son,' Dad yelled at him and Ray said, 'I been thinking da same thing, old man.'"

"That must've made your dad crazy!"

"Uh-huh, and it got worse. Ray just wouldn't shut up. 'A real dad wouldn't spend every damn minute preachin' at me,' he said. Then he gave this long speech about Mom and Dad being such great Christians, such super-Catholics, and how they blame him for every little thing."

Sal turned around and walked back out of the water and I followed him up the bank. He squatted and smashed some weeds with his fist. Then he sat the rest of the way down.

"Ray asked Dad why he never believed him. Like about the fight. He said the other guy punched him in the gut before he even touched him, but did Dad believe him? No. Then Ray yelled at Dad, 'An didja eva, jus *once*, forgive me for anything, Mr. Jesus Christ?'"

"Wow! He really said that?"

"Yeah. Then I heard somebody—Dad, I think—scoot his chair out, and I think he might've grabbed Ray by the arm or something. He said, 'Whether you like it or not, you're our son and we love you, but it's getting very hard to love this animal you're turning into!'"

Sal caught his breath and put his chin on his knees, like he was trying to remember what came next. Then he told me that Ray said, "You just love yourself—and maybe Mom and goody-goody Sal, but that's all.'

"I heard another chair-scooting noise, and I decided it was probably Ray's. I was ready to run around behind the house in case he headed outside, but then I heard him again, still in the kitchen. 'I'll be gone by tomorrow,' he told Dad. 'You can rent out my damned room. I'm outta here!'"

"You think he meant it?" I asked. The thought of going to

the Salvadors and not having to watch out for Ray sounded great to me, but I tried not to let Sal hear that in my voice.

"He's threatened to move out before, but this was a lot worse. He stomped back to his room and slammed his door so hard I heard a crash. In a little while, I went inside and back to my room and there in the hall was my mom's *The Last Supper* picture, knocked down on the floor. The glass was all over and the old wood frame had come apart on one corner."

Sal got back in the water and I followed him. He said, "I could hear Ray talking on his cell when I sneaked past his room. Probably calling Roger or somebody. Maybe his girlfriend."

"Ray has a *girlfriend?*" I asked. What I really meant was, a *girl* likes Ray? I didn't think anybody could stand him, especially a girl. "I never saw him hanging around with any girl."

Sal was floating on his back. "You haven't seen him and Trini Mendoza? Maybe at her surf shop by the mall? She's liked Ray ever since they were in middle school. If he doesn't move in with Roger, he'll probably move in with Trini at her apartment."

"Wonder why she likes him," I said. I was floating around then, too, and I couldn't see Sal's face.

"Beats me. Maybe because he's okay looking. Big. Tough. Girls like that, some of um."

"Yeah," I said. "I heard that, too. They like the wild, dangerous guys."

Sal paddled away, and we didn't talk about Ray for a few minutes, but I kept thinking about the type of guys that girls liked. Would Honey go for a guy like Ray? Never in a million years! She was too smart and too nice. But Trini Mendoza? She was always nice to me, too. She was little and pretty, with short, shiny black hair, and she laughed and joked with us when Sal and me hung around her surf shop. Well, I hoped she'd smarten up and tell Ray to take a hike.

"Anyways," Sal finally said. "Ray's really gonna move out. He's packing his stuff. Dad told him to use the boxes out in the shed. He's really gonna do it."

"Too bad he's leaving all mad."

"He doesn't care."

"I know, but your mom and dad probably do."

"Hey, they still have me, right? The goody-goody kid."

I laughed at that. "Yeah. We can't all be perfect."

"That's why us Catholics have confession," Sal said. He stretched out on the grass and put his wet towel over his head. I could just see his mouth and nose—no eyes, no hair. "Wake me up if I'm getting sunburned," he said. "I need to sack out for a while."

I said okay, but I knew too much was going on at his house for him to fall asleep.

TEN

Nothing really exciting happened for the next couple of days, and I was okay with that. Sal told me Ray moved in with Roger Tafasau, who had his own place over by the river. I knew which one it was. It was a little plantation house like Sal's grampa's house, but more run-down. Sal said Ray had stayed at Roger's house lots of times.

Roger's dad had bought the house from the sugar company after the factory closed. Then Roger's mom divorced his dad and moved to Seattle or someplace like that, just took off and left, and Roger got the house after his dad died. Mr. Tafasau was picking *opihi* on the Anuhea Bay cliffs when this giant wave came and knocked him in the ocean. People paid tons of money for those little round shellfish things to serve at their fancy luaus, so guys like Roger's dad took big risks picking opihi.

By Thursday, Sal and me finally came up with a science fair project we were sure Mrs. Chong would approve of. It was on two of the factors for incubating eggs. We told her we'd test to see which made the most difference, humidity or temperature, but Mrs. C. told us that our experiment had too many variables and it would be better to limit it to one factor and test just one thing so we could measure how it affected the chicks' development. We decided on humidity.

We'd test which percent of humidity would be best—which one would make for the highest percent of hatchability. We had no problem getting fertile eggs, and humidity was something we could control in my dad's old incubator. He has a bigger, newer incubator now, and he'd already said we could use the old one.

So, Mrs. C. approved and we were all set. We'd done what we could on the Internet, so on Friday, we hit the Kahili library branch after school.

We found Honey there, talking to Mrs. Miura, the librarian. Honey waved when she saw us and came over to where we'd piled our stuff on the biggest table. Sal said, "Eh, Honey. You study da roosta, too, uh?"

"That'll be the day! I can't believe Mrs. C. let you guys do your project on roosters. Aren't you around them enough every day?"

"Nah," Sal said. "We live for da birds. Grow um, sleep wit um, study um, sing wit um in da mornings—'*whoo-hoo-whooo*'—eat um…"

Honey blinked her eyes. "You eat *with* them? Or do you *eat them?* Nobody really eats the roosters, right?"

"Of course they do," Sal answered. "They're skinnier and tougher than the hens, but they're meat. My grampa says that in lots of places, like in Bali, the bird who loses the fight gets eaten. The guy who loses the match tears the bird in pieces and gives it to the winner to eat for dinner. But the winner has to cook him a long time in a stew, cuz he's tough as leather."

Honey said, "That's just lovely, Sal. Just what I needed to hear." She looked at me and shook her head. "You guys do your research. I'm out of here." And she went back to the stacks. In a while I saw Amy come in, so I decided they were probably working on their project together, just like Sal and me.

I was kinda surprised when Sal found this big book with all kinds of scientific stuff about incubating chickens on the first shelf we looked at. The guy who wrote it was a poultry extension specialist, whatever that is, and Sal checked it out so we could take it home.

Two smaller books on the same shelf looked like more fun. One was about cockfighting in New Mexico and one was on cockfighting on Bali. I wanted to check out the Bali one to find out if what Sal's grampa said was true about eating the loser, but we had to stick to our topic. We did find some good stuff in articles in three magazines on farming and on breeding livestock, though, and Mrs. Miura let us copy them on her machine for free. She said she always liked helping young scientists.

When Sal and me were almost ready to go I saw Amy leave, so I went over and sat by Honey for a few minutes. I asked her if they'd found any good stuff, and she said, yes, it was worthwhile coming to the library. We talked—quiet, of course—for a little while, and I decided that coming there was worthwhile for me, too. I'd gotten to see Honey again.

She showed me what she and Amy were doing, and I think it was interesting, but I can't remember much about it. I got all busy looking at a curl that bounced around by Honey's ear when she nodded her head, and then at this really tiny gold plumeria earring she wore on that ear. I mean, she probably had them on both ears, but the other one was hidden behind her hair.

She showed me something in a book, and I watched her bubblegum-colored fingernail going down the lines when she read that part to me. Her fingernails were nice and neat, like everything else about her. Nice, neat, and pretty. Her eyes smiled when she looked over at me.

"I'm glad you're interested in this, too, Paulie," she said, and I felt guilty. You know, like when your teacher praises you for answering a question right and it was just a lucky guess? But when Honey said, "I'm glad you have more than one dimension," I knew just what she meant, and I really liked hearing that.

"Yeah. I hope so," I said. "There's more to life than roosters, huh?"

"Lots more." She waited a little while before she said, "Does it ever bother you that you're involved in cockfighting, Paul?"

"I'm not really very involved," I said. "My dad raises really good roosters and sells them. It's a kind of work he can do with his back and leg problems, that's all. He doesn't fight his birds. Doesn't even go to the fights, that I know of."

"And what about you? And Sal? You ever go?"

"Nah. Sal's grampa Alberto would probably love it if we

went sometime. Ray thinks we should, too, but we probably never will. Ray says we're too big of wusses to watch even one match, let alone a whole derby."

She nodded. "That sounds like Raymond Salvador. I don't know him very well, but I'm not surprised he'd measure things that way. Anyone who doesn't like cockfights can't be brave. Can't be a 'real man.'"

She looked right into my eyes then, and I could tell that she was going to say something important.

"Paul," she said, "please promise me that you won't ever try to be like Raymond Salvador. Because if you ever did, I don't know how we could be friends anymore."

I kind of gulped, then I said, "Don't worry. I can promise that, easy. I don't even *think* like Ray, and I sure as heck don't want to *be* like him. I don't like the idea of cockfighting any better than you do." Then I added, for some reason, "And my dad doesn't like cockfighting, you know. He's not that kind of person, either."

Before she could say anything about that, I saw Sal coming over to drag me off to the bus. "Well, laters!" I said, starting to get up.

Honey touched my arm and smiled at me. "Yeah, laters, Paul. We'll get together soon, okay?"

"Sure thing," I said.

I hoped Sal and Mrs. Miura didn't notice I had this big, stupid grin on my face when I walked out of the library.

ELEVEN

On Saturday morning, Sal came over to work on our project. With Ray living at Roger's, we could've worked over at his house, but Sal's computer was way slower than mine. We didn't have any distractions, either, because Mom and Dad took off after the breakfast dishes were done. They were going to a weekend Marriage Encounter thing that the church was running on the other side of the island. It was supposed to make good marriages even better, Mom said.

I thought the retreat was a great idea because for the first time ever, I got to stay home by myself. I didn't have to go someplace with other adults like Emily did—she was staying at her friend Ariel Chapman's house all weekend. It took a while of telling Mom and Dad how responsible and mature I was, but they finally said we'd try it. Then they even decided that responsible, mature Sal Salvador could stay here with me because his mom and dad would be at the encounter, too, so I was really stoked!

Dad fed the roosters and checked on everybody before they took off, and Mom clamped this long list of stuff for me to do under the orange hibiscus magnet on the fridge. Uncle

Porky was set to come over for a while both days, but that was the only time we wouldn't be by ourselves.

Before Mom left, she gave me a kiss and asked, "Are you going to miss us?" Smart-mouth me, I said, "Sure, Mom. I'm gonna have to put my food in the microwave all by myself." And she said, "And that's it?" and she acted all heartbroken, but she and Dad were both grinning when they went out the door.

Emmie, who followed them out to the car with her little suitcase and her big doll, said she wouldn't miss me one teeny, tiny bit. *I* grinned about that.

So Sal and I were by ourselves, being responsible. Before we started to work, though, we went through the cupboards and fridge to see what junk food might be in there. Just so we'd have strength for doing our project.

We found corn chips, a couple of different kinds of Japanese *arare,* some pickled mango seeds, and other Chinese seeds. Believe it or not, with the papayas and carrot sticks and other healthy stuff in the fridge, we found two six-packs of Pepsi my mom must have gotten for us. We each grabbed a can and took the corn chips, seeds, and Japanese rice crackers back to my room.

After the snack we dug in to the incubation experiment stuff, and by ten-thirty we got to be experts on everything from cleaning and storing fertile eggs to knowing which was better, forced-air or still-air incubators. Dad's old incubator, the one he said we could use, was a forced-air kind, which was best because the eggs would get air circulated around them.

"Man," Sal said. "I didn't know this was so complicated."

He held up the book he'd been reading. "Listen to this. 'Store the eggs small-end-down and slanted at 30 to 45 degrees. Do not store for more than ten to fourteen days. After fourteen days of storage, hatchability begins to decline significantly.'"

"I knew that," I said. "Dad showed me most of this stuff already." I picked up a paper we'd copied at the library. "It says here, though, 'Of the four factors of major importance in artificially incubating eggs—temperature, humidity, ventilation, and turning—humidity tends to be overlooked, and that causes hatching problems.'"

"We're so good!" Sal said. "We decided on humidity even before we read that."

We figured we'd have time to hatch three batches of chickens before our project was due. Then we settled on testing out three levels of humidity for our experiment—65, 75, and 85 percent—to see which of those humidities made for the best hatchability. In plain English, hatchability meant the percent of the fertile eggs that actually hatched into live chickens.

"Mrs. Chong will *have* to like this," Sal said when we'd gotten everything written up in the computer. "It's so scientific." We celebrated with more Pepsis and a whole package of *li hing mui* seeds. Then we went out to check on the birds.

"Nice fence," Sal said.

"You saw it before. It's been finished for a while."

"Yeah, I know, but I didn't really look at it. Think it'll keep the boars out, though? Mom saw a gigantic pig sniffing around our mango tree. He might've been your boar."

"This is a pretty strong fence," I said. "But Dad said it was only temporary, anyway."

"So maybe he'll build a stronger one later?"

"I guess. Or maybe he meant that the whole thing with the roosters was only temporary." The second those words came out of my mouth, I wondered where that idea could have come from. Dad never complained about having to raise roosters. He didn't seem gung ho about it, but he didn't mope around after he lost his job and started up with the birds. If he wasn't happy, he only talked with Mom about it. They talk a lot about things they don't tell Emmie and me.

I knew Dad liked the pedigree charting and the testing combinations of foods and vitamins and deworming medicine, stuff like that. He could've done our incubation experiment with a blindfold on. He'd invented a wet-bulb thermometer that was better than any you could buy, and I told him he should sell them on E-bay, they were so cool. He said maybe he'd take my advice on that someday. He loaned us one of the bulbs to help regulate the humidity for our experiment.

Sal headed for the infirmary, so I postponed thinking about my dad and the roosters. We gave the incubator an extra good cleaning, then we sterilized it. We checked on the brood hens that lived on the other side of the infirmary. Their nests were full of clean, dry litter. We'd done about all we could then. Dad had said we should wait until Monday to collect the first batch of eggs we needed for our experiment. We'd need a dozen each time.

Our moms and dads had said we could go to a movie, so

after lunch we took the 1:35 jitney down the hill when it finally came at about two o'clock.

The Last Samurai was still in reruns at the Ilima Theater, and we'd heard it was a great guys' movie. I figured it was my kind of movie from seeing the trailers, but when Emmie said she'd never go see it in a zillion years with all those warriors getting hacked up with swords, I knew for sure it was perfect for Sal and me.

TWELVE

The movie was pretty cool. Not just all bloody with people getting hacked up. It had a lot of stuff about honor. Sal and me talked about it, going back home, and we gave it a good rating.

"Three and a half stars," Sal said. "I could've given it four, except for the ending."

"Yeah. That was *so* lame! If the guy really did understand about the samurai code of honor by then, he wouldn't still be alive."

"And he wouldn't be walking back to that little village," Sal said, after he thought about it for a minute. The jitney's tires clunked hard into the ruts in the dirt road. "And seeing the woman who took care of him all the time he was getting well after he got those sword wounds, and probably living happily ever after with her there."

I saw the picture in my mind. The little village was beautiful. The Japanese lady was beautiful, too. It was the ending you wanted, but it reminded you that what you watched was just a movie, not what really would have happened. "He should've been killed or killed himself on the battlefield," I said. "That's what a real samurai would've done."

"That's what a real man would've done."

"I probably wouldn't have done it, though," I decided. "I'd have chickened out."

Sal laughed. "My grampa says people who know anything about chickens never use 'chickened out' like that. Roosters are lots braver than people."

"Braver than me, that's for sure."

We started talking about other stuff then, like what my mom had left us for dinner, which was leftover pork teriyaki my dad barbecued for last night's dinner. I knew how to use the rice cooker, and I had it all ready to switch on the minute we got back. There were vegetables for salad in the fridge, but we decided that the stir-fried ones Mom left in a container would give us enough nutrition. Besides, we weren't starving because of all the popcorn we ate during the movie previews and stuff.

When we got home, we did a last check on the chickens while the rice steamed. They seemed to be settling down okay, and we could tell that Uncle Porky had come by when we were at the movie. No eggs were in Dad's big incubator, so we didn't have to worry about that. This staying-home-alone-and-being-responsible stuff wasn't bad at all.

Dad phoned when we were eating. Things were okay where they were, too. They weren't supposed to be calling people during the retreat, but Dad had borrowed somebody's cell phone to check on us.

"Sounds like your mouth is full, huh?" he said. "Well. I'm

glad everything's okay. Porky came over?" And I said, yeah, he had, and Dad said good and they'd be back about seven tomorrow night, maybe sooner. "Call Porky if you guys need anything," he added before he hung up.

But when we did need something—when we *really* needed something—there was no way we could let my Uncle Porky know.

* * *

We stayed awake almost all night talking and playing games and stuff, so we slept in too long Sunday morning to get the bus down to church in time for Mass. We were sure our folks would understand that. And when we talked about it, we were pretty sure that God would, too.

At about two in the afternoon, though, while we were watching TV, the roosters sounded a warning.

"A boar, you think?" Sal asked. We both jumped up and headed for the front door. But before we got outside, we heard a sound a lot worse than a boar's grunt. "Oh great," Sal said in this low voice. "That's Ray. That's his van."

Sure enough, Ray's green van was plowing up the dust on our driveway.

"Why's he here, Sal?"

Sal shook his head. We saw Ray climb down out of the driver's seat. He had on this bright yellow soccer shirt he always wears. Roger Tafasau jumped out the other side.

"Maybe he's here to see my dad," I said.

"Yeah. Maybe to buy a bird. Something like that. No way

he could know we're here by ourselves. And he wouldn't just come for a visit."

Kenny Aguilar hopped down out of the back of the van and the three of them stood around for a minute, then went over to the fence. They pointed to different birds and nodded and stuff.

"Yeah," I said. "Probably here for business."

After a while, Ray saw us on the front lanai and he gave a little salute. We waved back. "I think they're in a good mood," Sal said, without moving his lips. "But not drunk or anything."

The guys headed up to the house. "Hey, baby bro!" Ray said to Sal. "Decided we'd geev you and your bud here one beeg treat today." He turned back and said to Kenny, "You tink we should take um, Kenny? Was you idea, eh?"

Kenny said, "Eh, why not?"

Sal cleared his throat and asked, "Take us where?"

"Up Wainiha," Ray said. "Da Sunday Masses ova now. Time fo mo worship."

Kenny laughed like crazy. "Yeah. Roosta worship. Like da Grampa Salvador, huh? Good one, Ray. So I tell um, okay?" Ray nodded and Kenny said, "Lock up da house, kiddies. We takin you to one real life derby. You gotta know what one cockfight derby like, right? An Wainiha da bes kine."

"Lock up, Paul," Ray repeated. When I didn't move, he shouted, "Now! Gotta be up Wainiha fo da last matches in about..." He looked at his big silver watch. "Hell, we need go now. Go!"

"I have to tell my parents," I said in this tiny voice.

"Da parents gone," Kenny said. "No can reach um at da 'Encounter,' right, Ray?"

I grabbed Sal's arm and pulled him all the way to the house. "How'd they know that?" I muttered. But I knew. The Coconut Wireless. Everybody on this island knew everything. Damn! "We hafta do something," I whispered to Sal.

I turned around. "Raymond?" I called. "We'll just go to the bathroom, okay? Then I'll let Uncle Porky know where we're going."

That brought a big laugh from the guys. "No time, kid," Ray said. "Jus lock da house. Can pee in da trees, if need, like dese guys. He waved his hand around at Roger and Kenny. "Go to da *bat*-room, go to da *bat*-room," they chanted. They were having lots of fun.

Inside the house, I tried to think what to do. I told Sal to lock the back door from the inside. When I was getting the key from the kitchen basket, I picked up a pen and started a note to leave by the phone. I just got to "Ray's taking us to a—" when I realized that Ray was right there in the kitchen.

"You neva know wat 'hurry' mean, Paul?" I felt his hand clamp down on my shoulder and dropped the pen. "You guys act all *huhu.* Hey, dis one ex-*peer*-ee-unce. One Ex-*peer*-ee-unce of one Lifetime! Lock da front door and get in da van wid Kenny."

Sal had come in the kitchen in time to hear what Ray said. I saw his face and could tell he felt exactly how I felt.

Quick, though, he turned on this big smile for his brother. "Okay," he said. "We're ready to go now. Right, Paul? Yeah. One ex-*peer*-ee-unce!"

A minute later I had our house key in my shorts pocket and we were heading for the van. I was so, so glad it was light out. Sunny and bright. Because when Ray opened the door, the van smells hit me and my nightmare flashed in my head. My stomach felt sick. I took a deep breath of fresh air before I climbed inside.

At least it isn't dark, I thought. And I'm not all tied up and getting dragged to the van like in the dream. It's light, and nothing bad is going to happen. We're going to a cockfight, not a samurai battle where we'll get all hacked up. Ray's right. I've got to quit acting like a wuss.

Kenny plopped down on a rusty old lawn chair behind the driver's seat. He motioned for us to sit on the *lauhala* beach mats on the floor. "Come in, come in, keiki! Get da place all to ourself today. No roosta cage. Today, we jus bet. No fight, uh? An treat you keiki to a day out wid da real men. One initiation! Yeah. Today, you get one in-itchy-*a*-shun, big time!"

Sal and me grabbed for the walls when Ray threw the van into reverse and we lurched down the driveway.

Sal still had a smile plastered on his face. "And we're off!" he said to Kenny.

"You one good keiki, Sallie," Kenny said. "Neva had one brudda. Kine-uh miss dat, huh?"

Sal curved his mouth up a little more and said, "Jus aks Ray. He geev me to you, no problem."

Kenny smiled back. "Yeah, yeah. Ray git ridda you in maybe two second!" He turned to the front to see if Ray had heard, but Ray and Roger were talking. The only thing we could hear from the front seat was when Ray swore really loud at something.

We turned right after a while, up into the old lava flows, I guessed. All I could see was parts of ohia trees when I looked way up at the little windows. I might as well have had a blindfold on, because I was totally lost already. I just wanted to get out of the van before I threw up all over the floor, which would stop everybody from smiling so much.

THIRTEEN

The road Ray finally turned on got bumpier and bumpier, and that didn't help my stomach at all. Every time he tried to steer around a rough spot, Sal and me slid around on the mats. Sal looked like he wasn't feeling too good, either.

Kenny held onto the seat of his chair with both hands every time we dropped down in the potholes. When we hit a really huge one, his head almost hit the top of the van and he said the "S-word" real loud. "Sorry," he said to us. "Dat was one beeg bugga of a hole!" He rubbed his rear end from where he'd landed hard on the chair. "Auwe! Wen bus my okole!" he said. We all laughed.

After what seemed like maybe half an hour, Ray slowed down and I could smell some better smells coming in from outside—much better than the ones in the van. Smoke from Korean barbecue—kalbi ribs, it smelled like—and then barbecued chicken, and maybe some fish. We went even slower, and before we took a hard right turn and bumped to a stop I heard voices, closer and closer, laughing, teasing each other, some yelling, mostly guys' voices.

Sal opened the door and jumped out the second we stopped. He reached up and gave me a hand. When I thumped down on the red dirt, he was shielding his eyes from the sun and taking in the scenery.

"Paulie," he said. "Look where we are!"

I looked around and didn't see anything familiar. "I don't think I've been here before," I told him.

"No...I mean, just look at this place! It's like a carnival or something is going on here right in the middle of the trees. It's so *cool.*"

My eyes had adjusted to the light by then, too, and I saw what he meant. We were parked in the middle of a whole bunch of trucks, big ones with lots of chrome trim that were still shiny in the sun, even with all the dust, and big four-wheel drives. I couldn't see one sissy little Nissan or Toyota or even any regular-size cars.

In front of us, a whole field was cleared out in the middle of the ohia and eucalyptus trees. Tall Norfolk pines that looked like guards stood along the outside of the clearing, and there were real guards there, too—guys in gray security guard shirts who leaned on a fence that went around...well, it looked like a whole little town inside there. There was a gate to go in, with about twenty people standing in line on our side of it. A big Samoan lady who looked like Mrs. Faumina, our old school bus driver from grade school, was collecting money from everybody when they went in.

It did look pretty cool, like a big party, and between where we parked and the gate, at least fifteen food booths were set up under blue tarp tent covers. That's where the smoke came from: the long barbecue grills where women and a few kids turned over great-smelling *huli-huli* chickens, kalbi, steaks, Portuguese sausages, hamburgers—tons of food. The kids were scooping macaroni salad and rice onto big Styrofoam trays, ready for the meats when they came off the grills.

The ladies had grocery bags for the huli chicken halves, too, and when the chickens were cool enough to not melt the plastic bags, they'd get dropped into the sacks and somebody would buy them just as soon as they were ready.

My stomach was feeling lots better and I said, "Let's just stay out here, Sal. You can buy anything you want to eat here. Did you bring money?"

Sal looked at me like I was crazy. "Hey, I didn't know we were going anyplace, remember? We got *kidnapped*, remember? Besides, I already spent most of my money on the movie and the popcorn. You owe me for the popcorn, you know. You didn't pay me back."

"I didn't bring my wallet either," I said. "Guess we'll starve here, even with all the good food all over the place."

Ray and Junior had already picked up two six-packs of Budweiser, and they handed Kenny a can.

Roger popped his beer open and took a few swallows. "Ahh...perfect! Ice cold," he said, then he let out this huge, champion burp. "Well, men," he said, looking over his beer can at Sal and me, "Howzabout one nice, cold beer?"

I shook my head, but Sal reached his hand out.

"Why not, uh?" he said. "You thirsty, too, Paul?"

The guys laughed like crazy and Ray slapped the back of Sal's hand. "Mebbe ten years, you babies can drink. Now, fergit it. You get sick before even one match. You crazy, Roger? All-time cause trouble. Get couple dollas, Sal?"

Sal shook his head, and Ray said, "Sheesh!" He took a fat, worn-out denim surfer's wallet out of his back pocket and pulled out a five-dollar bill. "Okay," he said, "Get soda. Go."

Ray was really being nice. Everything was nice. This was a party, and I felt safe again, and happy, and kinda stupid for being so afraid to come here. This was all so cool!

I went with Sal over to this tiny Filipina lady who had more wrinkles on her brown face than even Grampa Alberto. She sat under a tent made of stretched-out sheets, in the middle of four huge ice chests. Before we even said anything, she pulled out two cold Pepsis and handed them to us. Ah...this was so much better than staying home all Sunday afternoon!

We looked through the slats of the wood fence and slurped our sodas. I could see part of a round ring that was dug into the ground inside there. It was surrounded by men, walking around and shouting numbers and making motions with their hands that I didn't understand. Well, this was our initiation day. In a while, I figured, we'd know all about this secret language.

The ring was close to the gate, but I couldn't see what was going on in the middle of it because lots of people were standing and squatting around the edge of the circle. I could see what was on the other side of it, though, up on a little hill. A bigger ring was cleared out there with four or five levels of wooden bleachers around some of it. My heart started beating faster because I knew that the big ring was what we were really here for. That had to be the cockpit.

Ray waved for us to get in line with them, and when we did, Kenny reminded him that, except for the Waiele derby, he'd been really lucky at the fights lately. "You should treat everybody," he said. Ray grumbled, but he finally said okay.

The lady who took the money really *was* our old school bus driver, Mrs. Faumina, but I don't think she recognized Sal and me. "Hey, Ray," she said. "Babysit da keiki today, uh?" She smiled down at us and pounded Sal on the top of his baseball cap with her big fist. Sal just looked totally embarrassed. "No charge fo da keiki, okay? Firstime, uh?"

Ray said yeah, and when the bus driver lady was counting out his change, he said, "Tanks, uh, Mabel. I tink, bout time da guys get one initiation."

Mabel laughed the big laugh like a man's that I remembered from when I took the bus in third grade. "Sure ting, Mr. Ray. Let um in, Herman," she said, and this huge sumo-wrestler-looking guy waved for us to go inside.

FOURTEEN

I'd heard roosters from outside of the fence but couldn't see any because of all the people. Ray, acting like Mr. Bigshot, pushed his way through the crowd so we could see what was going on in the smaller ring. "Da keiki like see, okay?" he kept telling people, and when they saw Sal and me, they let us through.

In the middle of the smoothed-out dirt circle, there were tons of roosters. I knew the names for some of them—Clarets, Hatches, Roundheads, and White Hackles mostly. Some were in traveling cages like we had at home, and some were inside those pretty woven baskets with lids like I'd seen on Grampa Alberto's front porch.

A huge Miner Blue scratched in the dirt, his neck stretching his tether. Other roosters were staked around the ring where the men could check them out. They got measured and their wings got spread out to see how big they were. Guys checked to see if the birds had muscles under all those feathers and poked at them like papayas in the farmers' market.

Ray pointed to a man who'd just come into the ring. He was a fat, sweaty guy in an orange aloha shirt that wasn't big enough to get buttoned up in front. He was holding a red rooster on his hairy chest and stroking its hackles and talking to it like it was a baby. A smaller man carried a white bird just the same way, and the two guys said "Howzit" to each other like old friends.

"Sam Camacho," Kenny said. "Da beeg guy Sam Camacho. Will be champion, da Red. Will fight Manny Salvador bird. Hey! Sal. Manny you cousin, no?"

Sal, who'd been watching a guy in cowboy boots checking out a bird's legs, looked up. "Hey! Yeah. Second cousin, I tink. Yeah. Das Manny, okay."

"Maybe I bet on Manny scrawny roosta, den. Da White. You tink? You family."

By then, the men had put the roosters down at opposite sides of the ring and the birds strutted around, not even noticing each other. Sal moved a little closer and gave them a long look. "Nah," Sal said to Kenny. "Da White get too low a head. Look like he get one crooked foot, too, see dat? Mo betta you take da Red."

"Hey!" Kenny said to Ray, who'd just come from the back where he and Roger were talking to some guys. "Da keiki know all about da roosta an da betting. Some kid, uh? Smaat, dat, you brudda. I tell um he can come live my house, uh? You no need one smaat little brudda. I take um."

Ray shook his head. "You no like. He one lazy wuss, dis guy," he said, but he was smiling at Sal.

Sal looked pretty proud of himself, and I was happy that

Ray was finally being nice to him. Who knows? Maybe bringing Sal to a cockfight would make Ray feel more like a real brother should feel.

For a minute I felt sad about having just Emily, and not a brother, but then I looked at Sal and I knew that I didn't really need a brother. Sal was better than any brother I could ever have. And with him, I didn't have to take the chance of getting a real brother that turned out like Ray.

I was hearing numbers called out again, and Ray let us know how the betting was done. It's kinda complicated, but the guys who were laughing and swearing and making motions with their hands were all setting up bets.

"No contrack," Ray told us. "No need. No 'sign on da dotted line' crap. You lose, you pay. No need shake hans even. Get honor, das why." Sal and I nodded, learning our lessons in Mr. Bigshot's cockfighting school.

But then I asked a question that Ray didn't like. I'd been noticing men, and even some boys, over by the back side of the fence. They weren't laughing, or even talking very much.

"What are those guys doing?" I asked, pointing to a man taking some money from a kid who looked about the same age as me. "They betting, too?"

"You stupid or wat?" Ray asked me, leaning his face down close to mine so he didn't have to talk loud. "Das *pakalolo,* mebbee ice. Who know? An *nunna you business!*"

I should've shut up then, but I was so surprised I kept on asking questions. "They sell marijuana right here? They sell drugs right out in public? Isn't that illegal?"

Ray shook his head and gave me a real stink-eye look

before he stomped off to where Roger was betting.

"End of conversation, Paul," Sal said. "Didn't you notice that this is *not* out in public? The gambling, the drugs, the fights, none of this stuff's legal."

"Okay, Mr. Know-It-All," I said, bowing to him. "You can ask all of the questions from now on."

In a few minutes, Mr. Camacho and Mr. Salvador handed their roosters over to another guy who pulled their wings up above their heads so that he could clamp them on a white scale, the kind they use to weigh the fish you catch in a tournament. The man announced that there was only a couple of ounces difference in their weights, so the match was on.

The guy standing next to me said, "Camacho neva handle his own roosta. Roberto handle for da red bird, an new guy name Alfred fight da White for Salvador." Sure enough, a guy in a green golf shirt had picked up the Red from the scale and calmed it down. The white rooster's handler, a short guy in a mostly brown aloha shirt, grabbed the other bird after he got weighed.

A loud cowbell clanged from over in the big ring, and people started heading to the bleachers. Ray shoved us along and we ended up in pretty good seats. I looked around for Sal, but he wasn't there.

Then I spotted him. He'd ended up sitting with Roger and Ray about four rows above me. I couldn't even turn around and signal him or anything without getting my neck all out of whack. Kenny sat down next to me. Oh, well. If I had to choose, Kenny was better than either Roger or Ray.

Kenny pointed toward a Hawaiian man at the other side

of the ring, standing in front of a timer, a huge clock with just one black hand on it. "Da ref," he said. "What he say go. One bird run away or get kill, he da loosa. If bote da birds alive at da end, da referee decide da winna an dat's it. No question. No complain. Not like one soccer game, uh?"

"Nope," I said, "This isn't anything like a soccer game."

The roosters' handlers opened a wooden box and pulled out these things that looked like curved ice picks. The metal flashed in the sun. "Gaffs, huh?" I asked Kenny.

"Yeah. Make for betta fight, you know. Use da knife when want short fight, but gaff make *betta* fight. Knife fight sometime ova too quick, not even one minute, uh?"

I'd heard about that, and I was glad the handlers weren't attaching the long knives to the birds' left legs. Instead, they put on the gaffs over the stubs on the backs of their feet, which was all that was left of the spurs after they were filed down when the birds were younger. Then they wrapped something around it that looked like dental floss or *sugi*, the line I used for fishing. Wrapped it around and around the leg and the gaff.

"Gaff jus as sharp as knife, kid," Kenny said. "Like one razuh. All time da handla get slice up. Whew! Hard, dat job. I neva be one handla."

"Yeah, me neither," I said to my new teacher. "But why don't they just leave the natural spurs on? Those can do lots of damage. Why use the gaffs or the knives?"

Kenny frowned. "Dis way, no dis-advantage," he said. I thought for a moment, then I nodded to let him know that I understood. Roosters' spurs grew to different sizes, but I could tell from looking at them that the gaffs were all exactly the same. I watched the referee measuring the gaffs the handlers had chosen from the box. Good, I thought. If they were equal, the fight would be more fair, right?

Well, I decided, looking at the people there, this isn't too bad. I turned clear around and saw Sal, but he was looking the other way. A couple of seats over from him, though, I saw somebody else I knew. Old Father Guerrero, who used to be my mom's teacher before he retired about a hundred years ago. He was talking away to this guy sitting beside him. Wait a minute! I knew that guy, too—Mr. Peterson, who sold his orchids and anthuriums in the shop off Leinaka Street. Or at the pier when the cruise ships came in. These were regular people. Hey, no monsters here, huh, Paulie?

I looked back at the ring, and for a minute something inside of me wanted the fight to start. That didn't last very long, though, because everything else inside me wanted things to be just the same as now. Just sitting around with normal people, learning stuff from Kenny, maybe going back for another Pepsi or some kalbi.

The handlers each let their birds have a couple of pecks at each other while they held them tight. Then, before I could even take a breath or look away, the handlers swooped their roosters toward each other like airplanes landing and let them go. The birds put their heads down, sizing each other up, then they stretched themselves as tall as they could. The Red lunged at the White, and everybody started yelling and clapping. Kenny dug his fingers into my shoulder. "Yes!" he yelled. "Go, Red! Go, Big Red!"

But the White dodged like a prizefighter. Like lightning, he attacked, flying into the air, four or five feet up, his hackles up and his feet stretching out. His gaff slashed the Red's chest before he pulled away, and blood dripped onto the dust. Red and white feathers flew all over.

The birds circled each other like boxers and then flew at each other again, and I thought of Grampa Alberto saying it was like 'one dance, one ballet.' The colors all mixed together—rust, white, green, black—like dancers' costumes. Yes! It was beautiful.

But it was not a dance. When I focused my eyes, I saw two roosters who wouldn't give up no matter how hurt they got. They fought on and on, and it seemed like I might spend my whole life watching them. The White seemed to be winning, but every time the crowd screamed at the Red to not give up, he went on the attack again.

Then the white bird slashed at the Red's eyes and didn't miss. The Red shook, but he stood on his two feet in a pool of his own blood. He staggered around, blind, but he still fought, breaking the White's wing, and I couldn't take it anymore.

I bent over and looked down at my feet, at my blue rubber slippers, but I could still see the birds turning each other into hamburger while the ring got redder and redder, and I could smell blood and heat and sweat and men…and something else I couldn't quite remember.

I felt Kenny poke me. "Almos ova, Paulie, take one look," he said. I forced myself to look back at the birds. Or at what used to look like birds. The Red was down, part of his stomach hanging out, and the White was still pecking at him.

"Red's still alive," Kenny said, just as the White's legs crumpled and he thudded down beside his enemy.

The referee let the handlers pick up their birds, and they tried to get them ready to fight again. Here were birds, hardly even alive, and they were supposed to fight even more! I couldn't believe it! A guy came into the ring, stuffed the Red's stomach or lung or whatever it was back in and put a bunch of stitches in him, all in about twenty seconds. He cut the thread with a knife and put the rooster down to fight some more.

But when the birds stumbled close to each other, the Red turned around and staggered away. He wasn't dead, but I knew the fight was finally over. His handler picked him up by the head with one bloody hand and shook hands with the White's handler with the other.

The handlers' green and brown shirts were so splattered with blood, it looked like *they'd* been fighting, not the roosters. The green-shirt guy lifted what was left of the white bird over his head, and people cheered. He bowed low, with the bird held out in front of him.

"Da champion!" Kenny yelled in my ear. "I'll be damned! Shoulda bet on da Salvador bird! Get game. Get plenny heart! Das okay…was one great fight, uh Paulie?"

I tried to answer him. Tried to say that, yeah, it was really great! Exciting as hell! But nothing came out of my mouth. All I could do was watch the birds being carried out, winner and loser, and wonder how anybody could let them hurt each other so much, and not just my stomach felt sick. My whole self felt sick, and guilty.

I knew I could never watch anything like that again. Even more important, I couldn't be a part of it anymore. I had to do something to stop this stuff. Honey was right. Cockfighting was very, very cruel.

Right then I remembered that other smell. The one that made me feel really sick even though I didn't think I'd ever smelled it before. I think, in the middle of the cockfight, I was smelling how war must smell.

FIFTEEN

I don't know how I got clear outside of the fence before I threw up, but I made it. I didn't know if Kenny or anybody was following me, either. I didn't care. I ran into the trees in back and let it all come out. My lunch, the Pepsi, all of it.

After I'd pretty much covered up the little ferns on the ground, I stood back up again. I stripped off a big banana leaf and wiped my mouth with it. I felt kinda dizzy, but much better. Then, before I could turn around, somebody's hand touched my shoulder.

"You okay, little Silva?"

I hadn't seen Sal's grampa at the fight inside, but I knew it was him talking. I didn't want to face him. You just don't feel proud of puking your guts out in front of somebody, especially a guy.

"Yeah, I'm fine." I gave my mouth another swipe with the leaf and turned around. "I didn't hear you coming."

Grampa Alberto shook his head, then he pointed at his chest. "Small, das why. You no can hear cuz no weigh much." He smiled a little, but looked worried, too. I knew right away that he wasn't going to make fun of me.

"Guess it was the bumpy ride here in Raymond's smelly van," I said. "The Pepsis and stuff."

Grampa nodded. "You *pau* here?"

"Yeah, I'm done." I patted my stomach. "Nothing else in here to come out." I made myself smile. Even though I could tell the old man wasn't going to give me a hard time, I still felt pretty stupid.

I started walking back toward the fence and Grampa Alberto shuffled along behind me.

"Where'd you come from, anyway?" I asked him. "I mean, I didn't see you watching the fight."

He let out a loud sigh. "Nah. My bes fren, Alex, he spose to pick me up." He pointed over to another old guy who was standing just inside the entrance, talking with Mrs. Faumina. "We come early, huh? But get big problem wit da ole Buick. Blew one rod, Alex tink. Beeg money fo fix. So we call one udda fren to take us. Das why we jus get heah, huh? Miss everyting."

He turned to me and kind of squinted in the sun. "Was good match, dis one, little Silva?"

"Um...oh, yeah! Two really great fighters. White and red. Some guy from your family owned the winner, the big white bird. Manny Salvador? I think that's who it was."

"Ah. Manny, yeah!" He nodded his head like mad. "Good. Sal inside still?"

"I think so." I hadn't seen Ray or any of the gang coming out yet. Then it hit me. "Hey, how'd you know we were here?" I asked.

"Run into Ray girlfren, dat Trini. She tole me Ray had

some stupid plan, uh? She no was happy, dat girl, but what she gunna do, uh?" Sal's grampa put his hand on my shoulder again for just a second. "Well...good you okay. Nex time mo betta, little Silva." He headed over to his friend then. They talked for a minute, then Grampa Alberto gave me a low shaka sign and they left for the parking lot.

Too bad he came all the way over here and missed the fights, I thought. He really loves watching them. I heard his words in my head, kind of echoing. *Nex time mo betta, little Silva.*

There'd probably be a next time for him, and a next.

But not for me. Never again.

"Paulie! Hey!" A bunch of people had crowded out of the cockpit arena at the same time, and Sal was the one yelling at me. He gave me a salute with his fist up high in the air. "I wondered where you was!" he said, with this huge grin on his face. "Wen you come out?"

"After the fight." I was glad I hadn't made a stupid idiot out of myself by running out in the middle of all the blood and feathers.

Sal probably wouldn't have noticed if I'd left during the fight, though. He was too stoked to pay any attention to anybody else. "Paulie," he said, "wasn't that something? I could hardly believe it!" He flashed a grin at Ray, who'd caught up with him. Ray actually grabbed Sal's hair and gave it a friendly kind of shake, just the way a brother would do it.

I think that was the first time I noticed they kinda looked alike. Well, at least like brothers. It was mostly the grins and the same shaped eyes, all lighted up and excited.

For some reason, that didn't make me feel all that great.

I shook my head and tried to remember what Sal's question was. Oh, yeah, the fight. "Really something, yeah," I said. I wasn't lying, really. But then Sal reached out and grabbed a bunch of *my* hair and gave it a happy shake. "Isn't it great, Paulie?" he said. "Wasn't it just like my grampa said? Beautiful, and exciting as hell!"

That was when I lied to my best friend for the first time I could ever remember. "Yeah," I said. "It was a great fight, for sure. As exciting as hell!"

I was glad that I was already through throwing up, because when I heard my voice say that, and saw Sal and Kenny high-fiving each other just like nothing rotten had happened, I felt sick again.

SIXTEEN

I don't remember as much about the ride back home as I do about the one going up there, except that it seemed even longer because I wanted to just get home and run to my room and crash on my bed. Sal stayed excited the whole trip, though. He didn't even notice that I wasn't talking much. That part I do remember.

I couldn't believe it. Sal? Loving the fight? What was going on? I knew already that deciding I had to take a stand on the whole cockfighting thing wasn't going to be easy. But what was with Sal? The same kid who'd just about cried when he saw his hurt bird? My friend for a hundred years?

Maybe watching the fight changed us both. Just not in the same way.

Anyway, we finally got home. Not my home, of course—we got dumped out at the bottom of Sal's driveway. Ray pulled just far enough into the drive to back up and get himself turned around on the road again. Then Roger gave us a wave from the side window before Ray gunned the engine and peeled out. Sal started toward his house but I just stood there, dust whirling all around me.

"Hey, Paulie! Come on in and I'll find us something to eat. Nobody's home still. Probably not at your house, either."

"Uh...thanks, uh? I think I'll head on home. Kinda tired, you know." I shuffled a foot around in the dust.

"Oh, sure. Yeah. Guess I'm kinda pooped, too. After all the excitement and stuff. Maybe later. Yeah. Come over later on, okay?"

"Sure," I said, trying to sound like my normal self. "Probably. Well, laters, man." I'd said "probably," so that one wasn't a real lie.

* * *

Sal was wrong about nobody being home. As soon as I turned onto our driveway I could see our car in the carport. Suddenly I really was tired, like I'd told Sal. Maybe I could just go around to the back door and they'd think I'd been in my room all the time.

But no such luck. Mom was looking out the window, and before I even got to the house Dad was out on our front lanai asking me where I'd been.

For a second or two, I almost said, "Over at Sal's," but this was my dad asking.

"Ray came and picked Sal and me up," I said.

Dad stared at me. "He did *what?* You guys went somewhere with Raymond Salvador?"

"Yes, but we—"

"You know you weren't supposed to go anywhere except to the movies. Let alone with..." He pulled the door open and motioned for me to go in.

Mom was standing there in the living room watering her African violets, but when Dad said, "They went someplace with Raymond," she put the plastic pitcher on the floor and went over and sat down on the sofa.

"Can I go to the bathroom?" I asked.

Mom blinked a couple of times and said, "Yes. Of course," so I did, and after I flushed, I grabbed the green mouthwash out of the bottom cabinet and swished some around through my teeth until I felt like I was ready to go back. I walked really slow.

Dad was sitting by Mom. He cleared his throat and spread his fingers out on his knees. "So, Paul," he said. "Can you tell me what happened?" He seemed pretty calm, but Mom was looking at me like I was somebody else's kid.

Then both of them started talking at the same time. "What in heaven's name possessed you to take off with Ray Salvador, of all people?" "All we saw when we got home was part of a note on the notepad and we were worried sick." "Ray Salvador, of all the people in the world!" "Where did he take you, son?"

That last question was from my dad, and, boy, did I try to think of a way to not answer it. I sat down on the big *koa* rocking chair, for the first time noticing how small I was in it. "Sal and me didn't…I mean…well, they came and picked us up in the van. Ray and Roger and Kenny."

"And?" my dad asked.

"They weren't drunk or anything. They decided it would be a good time to take us to a cockfight, I guess. Anyway, that's where we—"

"Oh, dear Lord," Dad said.

Mom put her hand over her mouth. She didn't say anything, but she was looking at me like she was going to cry or something.

"We didn't want to go! And we were trying to call Uncle Porky but..." And then it all came out. Almost everything, anyway. About Sal and me getting kidnapped, kinda, and riding in the van. About Mrs. Faumina and the kalbi and the Big Red and Manny Salvador, and about seeing Sal's grampa and...well, I stopped just before the part about getting sick in the trees.

"So, Paul," my dad said at last. "It doesn't sound like you had much choice in the matter. But that Ray Salvador...I am just *furious* at this! He must have known you boys were here by yourselves."

"Yeah, I think so. He told his girlfriend Trini that he was coming to pick us up. Sal's grampa said she wasn't too happy about it."

Mom leaned forward. "Well, I can tell you someone else who's not happy," she said. "A *cockfight?* That's not a place you take children! Your father and I were..." She stopped for a second, then she got this weird look on her face, sort of like she'd thought of something funny.

"There your father and I were, over at the Marriage Encounter. Trying to learn how we could have a better marriage, be better parents." She shook her head. "And all this afternoon, one of our children was at a...at an illegal *cockfight,* where there were probably illegal drugs and who knows what all, and we didn't even know it!"

"Calm down, Julie," Dad said. He rested his hand on her leg. "This isn't anybody's fault. Paul got back safely. Maybe God had a reason for this."

"Well, if he did, I cannot *begin* to comprehend it."

With that, Mom stood up, straightened her muumuu, and walked out of the living room, not even picking up her plant waterer.

I tried to think of anything good that had come out of the day, but I couldn't understand what God had in mind, either.

Unless…I remembered what I'd promised myself. That I couldn't be part of the cockfighting business anymore. Was this when I was supposed to tell Dad about how I felt?

He was leaning his head back on the top of the sofa. He looked almost as tired as I was. And sore, too. When his back got hurt in the accident, it made everything else hurt, especially his neck. I stood up. I didn't need to talk to him today.

But Dad said, "Wait for just a second, Paul. I still have a couple of questions for you, okay?"

I said, "Oh, sure," and I straightened the red cushion on the rocker and sat back down.

"Just what were your impressions of the cockfight, son?"

"My impressions?"

"Yes. How did *you* feel about it? As you can tell, your mom and I were not planning to take you to a fight at this point. And I'm pretty sure that Sal's going to hear this same question when his folks get home." He glanced at his watch. "In fact, they should be home by now. So?"

"I felt bad, I guess. I didn't want to say anything in front of Mom, but I wasn't brave. I shut my eyes and tried not to hear or to breathe, but the fight was awful. It made me sick."

"You felt bad."

"Yeah, that, but I *really* got sick. When it was over I threw up in the trees in back of the first ring." I made my mouth smile. "I barfed all over a bunch of ferns out there."

"I'm sorry this happened, Paul, but it isn't something—"

He didn't finish because my mom came back in right then and asked him if he could pick up Emily.

"Sure thing," he said. "Want to keep me company, Paul?"

I said okay and went to the kitchen for the car keys. I tossed them and he caught them overhanded, then he pulled himself up out of the sofa and grabbed his cane.

I heard the roosters making quiet little sounds when we walked out on the lanai. Dad walked on down but I stopped for a second to look over the birds. The rooster yard looked like a neat little village to me—not anything like the cemetery Honey said it looked like. But I was starting to understand how she felt.

* * *

When we drove Emily home, she talked nonstop about what she and Ariel did both days, then she told us two new jokes (actually, very old jokes) Ariel's sister had told her. Both started with, "What's black and white and red all over?" The first answer was "An embarrassed zebra." I knew the other was probably "A newspaper," but Dad and I said we couldn't guess, so she had fun explaining the red/read thing to us.

Emmie's chattering lasted clear through dinner. That kid

is amazing. There was no talk about anybody else's day, but I did get a few words in about the movie when Emily wound down. No jokes, though. Just samurai stuff.

Mom and Emily took their bubble baths and went to bed early. Dad had spread out the Sunday paper on one end of the kitchen table and I did my math assignment on the other end. We didn't talk for a while. Then we both put our stuff down and stretched and yawned at exactly the same time. We laughed, but didn't get up.

"You hungry for dessert now?" I asked Dad, and when he said yes, I sliced two big pieces of mango bread from a loaf some lady at the retreat gave Mom. While we ate, I told Dad I was sorry about making him and Mom so upset.

"I promise, Dad. That was *not* what Sal and me planned for this afternoon."

He smiled and put his fork down. "I believe you, and I know your mom does, too. We were both upset, but not with you. Really. So don't worry about it, okay?"

"I should probably just worry about getting sick there. I wasn't any braver than, maybe, Emily would've been."

"You had a perfectly normal reaction to all that you saw, judging from what you told us."

I shook my head, but I was glad he'd said that. "Have you ever been?" I asked him then. "To a fight? To a derby?"

Dad's eyes looked like he was remembering something. Then he blinked the memory away and said, really soft, "Yes. I was about your age. My dad took me."

I heard myself asking him the same question he'd asked me earlier. "So what did *you* think about it?"

"About the same as you, apparently," he said. "I didn't get sick as I recall, but I knew even then that it was a nasty business, the fighting."

"So then why are we doing this?" I pointed to our front yard. "All those birds out there, they're not waiting just to win prizes in the shows, Dad. Okay, a couple of um are. But you...*we* are part of this whole fighting business. Doesn't it bother you? About what happens to the roosters, I mean?"

Dad was quiet for so long, I almost backed up and asked him my questions again. Then he looked at me and I knew he'd heard. "I hate this just as much as you do, Paul."

There. He'd said it. Talking with him about this hadn't been so hard after all. I should have just done it before, and then our family's part in it would all be over by now. I was so relieved.

"So we have to stop this, right? When can we stop?"

I didn't expect him to say a date, like "next Tuesday" or something like that, but I sure didn't expect how he answered me.

"We can't, Paul."

"What do you mean?"

"If it was as easy as just deciding how things *should* have been, how I wanted them to be after the accident, I'd never have started raising the roosters. Yes, I get some satisfaction from taking care of them. I like breeding them so they'll be strong, and I'm a little bit proud of all the ways I've learned to keep the roosters healthy. But since I got hurt, raising gamecocks has turned out to be the only way I have for earning a living—until I'm okay again. Believe me, Paul, I've looked long and hard for other work that I can do while I'm recovering."

"But, Dad. Don't you even *care?*"

His eyes looked so sad, I wished I hadn't asked him.

"Of course I care, son. I've been torn up inside ever since those first hatchlings pecked their way out of the shells. Your mom knows this. You and I should have talked about it, too, I guess. You're old enough to understand and to have your own feelings about it."

Then I remembered some of the things he *had* told me…or tried to tell me, and I said, "I guess you tried. Maybe when we talked about the pig. And about this being temporary. And some other times." But that still didn't help me to understand, so I had to ask, "But we'll just keep on breeding and raising fighting cocks for forever? That's what you want to do?"

"It won't be forever. But that's all I can promise. I couldn't come up with another alternative after I got hurt, and the situation's still the same. Even worse than it was then. My disability checks, plus what your mom earns from her garden and her crafts, aren't enough to pay our expenses each month. Not the mortgage, not you kids' school—"

"But we don't have to stay at Kaukani, Dad! Emily and me, we could go to public school." I hated the thought of changing schools, but I'd made this promise to myself. We'd both have to sacrifice, that's all.

"It's not that easy, Paul." Dad scooted his chair back and stretched out his legs. Then he leaned forward, really slow, and rubbed his knees with the palms of his hands. "You'll have to trust me on this," he said. "Until I can find another job, an alternative to raising roosters, we're stuck with this one."

"That sounds like forever to me."

"Well, I hope not, but Dr. Graham says I'll never be able to work at the lumberyard again, not in my old job at Nakasone's, anyway. I've talked with Hideyo Nakasone about office work, but he says he's already overstaffed and he can't fire somebody just to make a place for me. I've looked around, called around. The job market here right now is terrible, especially for...somebody like me. Until I can find something else, this has to be my business. Can you understand this?"

"I guess so. But it's not fair, Dad."

"Lots of things aren't fair. You know that. It wasn't fair that the lumber shifted on the pallet and crushed me underneath it." Dad never talked about the accident, and he didn't say much more even then. He just said, "But I have to be grateful that I wasn't killed, right?"

The back of my neck felt cold. I'd thought about that, lots of times. And right then I remembered that I'd dreamed about it, too. And that when I woke up after having that dream I was even more scared than when I had the nightmares about Ray. I loved my dad. Lots of kids had no dads, or moms, and I had both, and they were good ones. I had to be thinking about the good things. I had to think positive.

"I'll figure out an alternative for you, Dad," I said then. I was absolutely sure he just wasn't looking hard enough. How could there not be one job that would be good for him to do that wasn't raising roosters?

"Sure, son. That's all we need right now. An alternative job, alternative income. Just enough money to supplement my disability payments and we should be able to make it."

"We'll do this, Dad. We have to."

He looked me in the eyes and he smiled. "You're something, you know. You've just about convinced me."

I knew we were done talking. I picked up our plates and forks and rinsed them in the sink while Dad got up. "What do you think of the mango bread?" I asked him.

"Not nearly as moist as your mom's."

"Yeah. Too crumbly."

Dad came over and hugged my shoulders before he went off to bed.

In a little while I was snuggled up in bed, too. I don't remember ever being that tired, but I stayed awake trying to think of a new job for my dad. How was I going to keep my promise? I thought about it so hard, my head and even my tongue and cheeks ached. How was I going to figure out what Dad hadn't been able to figure out, even though he really wanted to?

Finally I got calmed down by thinking about Dad getting well enough to do everything he wants to again. He's working so hard on the therapy, I just know he'll be that way again, and that will solve all our problems. So I thought about that and after a long time, I fell asleep.

SEVENTEEN

When I woke up, my alarm-clock rooster, #43, was crowing. I knew I'd miss him if we stopped with the roosters and Uncle Porky sold him off. Yeah, he was a squawky "beeg mout," but I liked him anyway. A couple of other guys started in crowing then, just like always, and things seemed okay again.

I opened my eyes and started thinking about Honey. She'd be happy with me when I told her what happened. What I'd decided to do. I think Honey knew what I was feeling all along. I thought I knew how I felt when I talked to her, too, but that was before the fight. Now, I can honestly tell her that our connections with the cockfighters will be over soon.

I wasn't too sure how Sal would feel about our wanting to get out of the rooster business, though. Probably surprised. I just hope he's okay with it, too, when we have a chance to talk.

On the way to school, Sal didn't say anything about Ray, or about yesterday. I was glad about that. Oh, yeah…he did just say his parents weren't very happy with him or with Ray when they found out where we went while they were gone.

Maybe that's why Sal didn't keep on saying how exciting the fight had been. Or maybe he'd been thinking about it, and he was starting to feel more the way I felt. I hoped that was it.

For most of the ride, we just talked about our science project. We were going to have to work more on it after we got back home from school. Collect the first eggs from the broody hens and wash and sterilize them and get them all set up in the incubator. Most of our research was done already, so the experiment itself—hatching the roosters, writing up our findings, and making the display—would be the fun part.

The first time I had a chance to talk with Honey was at lunch. I waited until she got in line at the cafeteria, and I got in right behind her. She turned around and said, "Hi, Paul. It's lasagna today. Not too bad, huh?"

"Yeah. Mondays. Usually it's not too bad on Mondays. Maybe Mrs. Cabrerra and her cooks have a good rest on the weekend so they plan some good stuff for a change."

Honey held out her plate and the lunch lady splatted some lasagna right in the middle of it. "Right," she said. "And then by Wednesday they're tired and take it out on us with the awful canned salmon stuff. Or what they call teriyaki, but it has that gruesome, really salty sauce."

The moment she said teriyaki, the smells from the grills at the cockfight came back. When Honey asked if I'd had a busy weekend, I said yes, and we looked around to find someplace to sit together, which we did. Clear in the back. Before I even started eating I gave her a condensed version of my

Sunday adventures. Not all the stuff she'd say was gruesome, but some of it.

Honey stayed quiet and just listened to the whole story. When I said, "You were right about things—it's pretty gross," she gave me this strange look. I thought she didn't understand what I meant so I said, "The fighting is pretty gross. Or at least the fight I saw was. We didn't get there in time for the others."

"What did you expect, Paul?" she asked.

"Expect? At the fight?"

"You really had to go to a cockfight to know what goes on?"

"Well…no. I guess I knew before. But now I *really* know. And I definitely don't want to be part of it. I kinda made this promise to myself."

I waited for Honey to smile. This was when she'd be happy with me. Good boy, Paulie. You've learned a valuable lesson, haven't you?

She took a little bite of lasagna and poked at her salad before she said anything. Then she said, "I thought I knew you really well, Paul Silva, but now I'm not so sure." She stacked her salad plate on her big plate, even though she hadn't eaten very much. Maybe I shouldn't have told her any of that bloody stuff during lunch. It's not too appetizing.

She pushed her chair back from the table and stood up. "Well, gotta go," she said.

When I saw she still had this sad look on her face, it hit me—maybe I didn't know her as well as I thought, either.

She looked down at my tray. "Better finish your lunch

before the bell rings, huh? You're probably hungry. You didn't get a chance to eat very much, having to tell me about…everything." Then she left.

Did I really know *anybody* anymore? First Sal, then my dad, now Honey.

I ate a little bit more of my lunch, then I scraped the rest into the garbage bin. The lasagna wasn't as good as it usually was today.

* * *

Sal came over after school and we went out to set things up in the infirmary. He was writing stuff down on a form that I'd put on a clipboard. Measurements for the incubator's humidity, starting times for the experiment, and things like that.

I was measuring the angles of the eggs in their containers when I said, kinda casual, "I think my dad and Uncle Porky should get out of the rooster business."

"You think *what*?" he said, sliding the clipboard back on the counter.

"Sorry. Just talking to myself."

"What kinda crazy talk is that? Stop raising roosters? You've got to be kidding! Your dad's about the best there is. Remember what my grampa said? 'One good breeda, dat Silva,' and if anybody knows his birds, it's my grampa. So what's up with this?"

I said I'd tell him later. We needed to concentrate on our experiment. We'd talk when we went back in the house.

After we finished our notes, we went inside and back to my room. We sat on my bed and Sal drank the last regular Pepsi and I had one of Mom's decaf diet ones.

I didn't exactly know how to start, so I talked a little about the drive up to Wainiha and about Kenny trying to teach me about the roosters when we were at the fight and stuff. Sal didn't interrupt me. He was a good listener, like Honey. But when I told him about how I really felt about the fight, he kept shaking his head and mumbling, "You've just *got* to be kidding."

"Nope. I should've been honest, Sal. The whole thing made me sick."

"Come on, Paul. It made me feel a little sick at first, too. But that's part of the excitement. You'll get used to it."

"No. I don't ever want to get used to it. I hate it. And that's what I told my dad. I told him that we had to get out of the rooster business."

"He laughed at you, right?"

"Wrong." I looked Sal straight in the eye. "He said he felt the same way."

"*Ho*...lee," he said.

"He wouldn't be raising chickens if he had any choice. But until he can find some kind of 'alternative job,' we're stuck with this one."

"*Stuck* with it? Paul, your dad's not crazy. His birds bring in good money. It's something he can do now while he's...disabled. Anyways, there's always gonna be fighting, so there's nothing he can do about that. It's been around hundreds of years. It's part of the culture—remember what my grampa told us? So your dad might as well make sure there are good, strong roosters to win the fights."

I closed my eyes. Sal was dead-on right about that. If we didn't raise the roosters, somebody else would. And a lot of people wouldn't treat the birds as well as we do. I opened my eyes. Sal was glaring at the floor, like he was fed up with me. I looked at his hair that curled just like Ray's. Their *ears* even looked alike! And now Sal was into cockfighting like Ray—he was defending it, even. Was Sal turning into his brother? A breeze came in my window, a cold one. I got up and shut the window, then I sat back down on the bed.

"The fights, Sal," I finally said, really quiet. "They're ugly and they're cruel. You know roosters can feel pain. Even chickens are living things...God's creatures—"

"Stop with the sermon already, Paul! That sounds just like something your dad would say. Or an old priest, maybe. God's creatures? They're God's creatures, okay, but God made um the way they are. The only feelings they have are wanting to protect their territory. So they were made to fight. They don't care if they get hurt. Or die. They're brave because they're made that way. And all our dads do is make um better fighters, so they can win the fights!"

By the time Sal said all that, he was standing up, waving his hands in the air. I knew he meant every word. I'd been wrong when I thought that everything we believed in was the same. Maybe when we were little kids, but now all of that was over.

I stood up, too, and walked with Sal to the door of my room. He stopped me there with his arm, though, and he walked down the hall. In a few seconds, I heard the front screen door close.

EIGHTEEN

That night I couldn't get to sleep for a long time again, but finally I did, and I slept really hard. No dreams, no noises waking me up, nothing that I could remember until I opened my eyes. It was still dark. I stuck my arm out from under the covers. "Fifty-six degrees," I guessed. We'd been having really cold nights lately, but this one might set a record for the season. I wanted to stay all curled up in my big Hawaiian quilt.

But the roosters were crowing, and they had kind of a different sound. Not waking-up crowing. More like gurgling kinds of crowing. I couldn't figure it out, so I made myself get up.

There was some noise in the kitchen, so I knew that Dad, at least, was awake. He's always the first one up, then Mom, then me. Emmie doesn't get up until you practically drag her out of bed by her feet. I couldn't hear talking, so I figured it was just Dad in there.

Most people think of Hawaii as hot, but it can get cold up here in the foothills. Not like on the mountains, of course, where it snows so much you can ski and the roads get blocked sometimes, but we get plenty of nights when it goes down into the fifties. My floor was freezing, so I grabbed my rubber slippers and put them on. Then a T-shirt and jeans, then this heavy sweater Auntie Sylvana knit for me. I wear it maybe twice a year, but it was on my chair because I'd worn it twice this week already.

It was Mom in the kitchen, not Dad. She heard me come in, I think, but she didn't answer when I said, "Morning." She wasn't making breakfast, just fiddling around with some of her wreath stuff on the table. When she looked up at me, I knew there was trouble.

"Your dad's in front," she said, and I headed outside.

It wasn't raining, but it sure felt icy out there. I pulled my sweater tighter and buttoned it while I crossed the lanai and walked down the steps. Good thing the moon was pretty big so I could see where I was going.

Dad was down by the roosters, on the infirmary side. I saw him kinda bent over in the yellow light from the camping lantern. When I walked down, slow so I didn't trip, I felt like I was seeing him with binoculars that were turned the wrong way around. It seemed like he got smaller and smaller when I got closer to him. I noticed how big his old flannel shirt was on him now. Almost like a nightgown. I wished more than ever that he'd not gotten hurt. That was so unfair.

The roosters were still complaining in that gurgling way that woke me up.

"Dad?" I said when I was close to him.

"Ah, Paul. I didn't hear you coming."

He moved the lantern so I could see the new fence. Two metal posts were bent almost together, and the middle chain-link part sagged just about down to the ground.

"Wow! Not a pig this time," I said.

"Nope. I thought I heard some commotion around three o'clock, but I was so tired I just pulled my pillow over my head and slept some more. In the back of my mind, I thought, yeah—maybe another boar. But I wasn't worried. We've got the fence now."

"Yeah," I said, trying to be cheerful. "I've never seen a pig able to jump five feet, huh? Even with a running start! But I don't get it. I didn't hear anything at all last night."

"This is a long way from your bedroom, Paul. It's probably just as well you didn't wake up. You might have gotten hurt." He pointed to the roosters' houses. "Two are gone. The Reds, here and here. The most valuable birds in the lot. I shouldn't have kept them right by the driveway. Too much temptation, maybe."

"But hardly anybody comes here."

"It just takes one, son."

I knew right then who that one was, but I didn't tell Dad. "Did you call the police?" I asked him.

"No need. They're gone now and there's no way to prove who did it."

"I'll find some proof. Nobody's gonna take your property—just walk in and grab your best birds!"

"Somebody already has."

Dad was standing inside the rooster yard, but I was on the driveway side of the fence. Instead of going back to the gate,

I scrambled over the sagging fence, just the way the thief had. He'd probably kicked and trampled the chain links clear to the ground, then just bounced over them like I did. Dad showed me the dirt around the holes where the birds had been tethered to the stakes. He handed me the lantern and leaned hard on his cane while I held the light close to where the birds had been. Just the stakes were there.

"Hey. Anybody home here?" I said, knocking on the roof of number 29's A-frame. "Anybody seen any birdnappers?"

Dad didn't smile. He walked away and stood by the fallen-down fence while I looked for clues. Anything. Footprints maybe, but the ground was dry and hard, and if the thief had trampled the grass, it had already popped back up. I checked the fence. Nothing.

I looked over by the other rooster's house. That was when I found it. I couldn't believe I noticed it, but there it was. Small, yeah, but definitely there. I pulled a tiny piece of shiny yellow cloth off of a nail head sticking out on the A-frame's roof. Shiny, gold-yellow material. Just a little shred.

I stuffed it in my pocket, then went over and handed Dad the lantern. I walked and half-crawled back over the fence and crossed the driveway, leaving Dad standing there. I grabbed my bike from its rack under the infirmary's eaves, turned it around, and jumped on. Then I took off down the driveway so fast that Dad probably didn't even realize what was going on until I was almost down to the road.

"Paul?" I heard him call. "*Paul!* Where are you going?"

NINETEEN

The light was getting a little better, but it would still be a long time before the sun would come all the way up. I saw shadows, mostly. I was pedaling so fast I should've crashed, but I almost floated down the hills toward downtown. There wasn't even one single car out, so I kept to the center of the road and even though I hit a few potholes kinda hard, I was down into town almost before I took a breath.

A record, I thought. A personal best! Paul Silva breaks the world record! And he's not even sure he wants to be riding today. He should screech to a stop now, turn around. But he's just turned onto the road that goes to the river and it's definitely too late to turn back.

I kept seeing my dad leaning on his cane, looking at the empty A-frames. Shrinking. Hurting. I had to do something. What, I wasn't sure, but I kept riding until I heard the river slurping and churning around up ahead.

I slowed down at the bridge. Then I stopped for a second to catch my breath. To check myself out. I wasn't as cold, but boy, I really should've gone to the bathroom before I took off. I pulled my bike over to the railing and leaned it there. I thought about peeing off the bridge, but if somebody came and saw me I'd croak. Instead I climbed down the mossy steps, holding onto the railing that was bolted to the lava-rock wall.

Everything was damp under there and dark, and the river sounded fast and crazy. Think about good stuff, I told myself, not what's really going on.

As I reached the rocks by the edge of the river, I heard Emmie's voice in my head telling her favorite joke. "Every little bit counts"—she'd wait a second before she'd finish—"said the old lady as she peed in the sea!" We'd all shake our heads and groan. Emmie would laugh like a hyena. She loved all her lame jokes.

I unzipped my jeans and added my little bit of water to the river. A lot, actually.

I got myself back together and realized that I wasn't shivering as much. The sole of my slipper snagged on something when I climbed back up the steps, but I caught myself. I held onto the railing like it was going to save me from falling clear down into hell.

I smiled and talked out loud when I was back up on the bridge. "Every little bit helps! Ha, ha, that's so lame, Emmie. I've got to teach you some better jokes." When I grabbed the bike's icy-cold handlebars, I stopped myself. I didn't say out loud what had just popped into my head, which was, "I'll teach you better ones if I'm still around to do it."

I should go home, I thought. Why make Dad more worried? And Mom?

But my foot found the pedal, and I rode over the bridge. I didn't let myself think until I saw the house about a half mile down the road.

Roger Tafasau's house was even more trashy looking than I remembered. Sal had mentioned that Ray talked about helping Roger fix it up when he moved down there, but it was still a mess. No plastic roosters like at Grampa Alberto's, but other stuff was spread all over the yard. I could see an old stripped car in front and bags of garbage piled into a small mountain on the closest side. The little bit of light that was now coming up from the ocean side was blocked by three or four huge mango trees. Their branches almost covered up the whole property.

I didn't want to go in that house.

Yes, I told myself, I did. I had to do something. I had to find Ray. If I was going to help my dad, if I was going to stop having nightmares about Raymond Salvador, I had to lay my bike down and walk up to that dark, still house.

I leaned the bike on a tree trunk. I took some deep breaths, then I threaded my way through the junk, being careful not to kick cans or something and wake up whoever might be in there. Halfway across the yard I had to stop taking deep breaths and start breathing through my mouth because everything smelled like cats had peed on it.

It had been cold up on the hill, but here it was worse because of all the trees, and being closer to the ocean. I thought I could see my breath in front of me when I got close to the little front porch. No, it couldn't be that cold. But my teeth were chattering and my knees shook when I climbed up the steps, quiet as a worm. A board creaked when I went over to look inside the window, and I stopped, but nobody yelled. I waited for a minute, then I put my slippers down flat and careful and I walked the rest of the way to the window.

I could barely see inside the dirty, spiderwebby glass, but my eyes adjusted, and there was Roger in the front room, sprawled on his back on a sofa. The louvers under the window were all open, and boy, was he ever snoring! I thought just old people snored, but Roger Tafasau was championship snoring material. I almost laughed, but then I remembered that I had to find Ray, and that wasn't funny.

Just as I backed away from the window and started to back off the porch, all of a sudden my head felt like it was swelling up. I pushed my cold fingers against the sides of my nose, but it didn't help. My stomach was okay, but my head felt awful. My throat started to feel itchy, and I got off the porch quick before I started sneezing.

I stopped for a second at the bottom of the stairs and looked up. Of course…the mangos! I couldn't see the furry-looking sticks of blossoms up there, but I knew the stupid trees had to be in full bloom. Pretty soon I'd be sneezing my head off. I definitely had to go back home. No way could I sneak around here with my allergy attacking me.

I walked back through all the junk to my bike. It was getting lighter out and the sky had the soft, pink-orange kind of light that comes about fifteen minutes before the sun's up all the way over the ocean. I turned the handlebars back and forth on my bike's new Shimono neck. Good old bike. Me and Sal were putting that neck on it last Christmas in his carport, but we had to stop because Ray yelled at us to quiet down. It was almost noon, but Ray was sleeping in. We ended up taking everything back over to my place to finish the job. Who knew when Raymond got up?

Raymond. He had to be in there.

I made my feet walk back, forced my legs to carry me along the side of the house until I reached the high windows where the bathroom was. If the house was exactly the same as Grampa Alberto's, there'd be a bedroom window...yes, there it was. I was just tall enough to look over the bottom of the windowsill.

Ray was there. Or at least it looked like him. The daylight hadn't gotten into the bedroom much, but a guy was in there, lying on his side on a bare mattress. His arms were out in front of him and he was all dressed. I stepped back. I was going to have to go inside. I'd come all that way. I had to do something about Ray.

In back of the house it was dark, almost like night. Something moved around by another junk pile. I froze. A rooster, maybe? Had Ray brought Dad's birds here? Nah. You don't muzzle a couple of roosters very easy, and I hadn't heard anything except for that skittering sound from whatever thing was back there.

Then the skittering came right at me and I almost screamed!

But it was just a stupid old mongoose, looking through the dumped stuff for something to eat, I guess. I was glad nobody saw me, all freaked out by a stupid mongoose. Just a mongoose. And no roosters.

I turned toward the back door and felt a breeze starting up, and then, "Whap!" I jumped again. The banging came from the door. I could see that it was open, and the wind had blown it, making the racket.

They'd left the back door open. Crazy guys. Anybody could just go in there if they wanted to.

I was going in there. I bent down and found a pile of rocks heaped around one of the stilts the house was on. I picked up a rock that was big and rough and black. A lava rock. It was kind of heavy, but I could hold it in one hand if I had to.

There was no porch in back, so I climbed up the three wooden steps, went through the door, and there I was inside, right by the bedroom.

I went in the room. It smelled like beer, and maybe dried-up sweat. My head wasn't getting any better, and I thought I might sneeze any minute, but my legs walked me right there inside the room. And there was Ray, lying on the bed, like I'd thought. Some of the beer smell came from a can that was right there by one of his clenched-up hands. Whatever he hadn't drunk had spilled out on the mattress.

I went closer. Tried not to breathe. I didn't want to smell Ray's smells. I didn't want to even see him, but some light was coming through the window and I saw his shirt, pulled part-way up his belly. His old, shiny *yellow* soccer shirt!

This was the idiot who stole our birds. Who always laughed at me and Sal, and used Sal's little rooster for bait in a cockfight. The guy who gave me nightmares, who forced us to go to the derby, and who made my dad's hurting even worse. He was right here, a foot away from me!

He wasn't moving. Maybe he was dead?

Then he took a big, snorting breath, and I knew I wasn't that lucky. I had to do something. I hated Raymond Salvador. Hated this guy with his big, whiskery chin and his hair curled on the mattress. My arm felt the weight of the rock in my hand. It was a good, big, rock. I could hurt him bad, show him what it felt like…

My throat and my nose itched. I can't sneeze now, I thought. If Ray wakes up and sees me, he'll kill me. I put a finger right under my nose and pushed hard, then clamped my teeth together, and it worked. I didn't wake up Ray.

There I was, standing over him with the lava rock in my hand, when something crazy happened. I started hearing voices talking in my head. I heard Sal and Dad and Mom, especially. The voices got louder than my own voice, and they were different from my voice. None of them had hate in them.

I heard Sal saying, "Hey…he's my brother." I heard Dad, sounding like that day in the infirmary when he said to pray for Ray Salvador because he was the one who needed it. Mom's voice just kept saying "No, no, no…," and then, real soft, "This isn't *you,* Paul."

Then I couldn't hear her. Couldn't hear anybody. I stopped looking down at Ray and shut my eyes. Shut them tight, but tears were still trying to push out. I was crying. Big, brave Paul Silva! Crying!

I turned a little and looked out Ray's window. I stood there for a minute, watching the trees moving and stopping myself from crying. The sky had gotten this wonderful gold color. A rooster crowed somewhere far away, and doves started up making their morning noises in Ray's yard.

I couldn't pray a very good prayer right then, but my lips moved and they said, "Help Ray," and then, "Help me, please," and I thought that maybe God would. He'd do something about Raymond, where I couldn't.

I put the black rock down on the mattress, right by Ray's head. I don't know why. Then I left.

TWENTY

I didn't get my sneezing fit until I was almost to the bridge. I sneezed over and over again and I finally had to get off and walk my bike. I was still sneezing when I saw car lights coming toward me from town.

Mom slowed the car down. She drove past me, then made a U-turn and came back to the bridge. Dad opened his window right by me and looked me over. He'd been worried, all right. I could tell. But he didn't yell at me. Just said, real calm, "So…you were looking for someone?"

I let out my breath. Twisted my handlebars back and forth. "Yeah. For Ray. At Roger Tafasau's house."

"And did you find him?"

I nodded. "He was sleeping. I didn't do anything. Just watched him. Then I left. The mangos have gotta be in full bloom. I've been sneezing my stupid head off."

Dad shook his head and looked over at Mom. She didn't say anything. I had this feeling that they might have had an argument about going out to look for me.

"Well," Dad said after a minute. "You want to ride your

bike back up, or put it in the back and let the car do all the work?"

"Guess I'll ride with you."

"Good. You need to eat something. Your mom made some eggs and French toast. And you still have to get ready for school."

Mom handed the keys over past Dad. I opened the back of the wagon and shoved my bike in. "The bike says thanks," I said when I was sitting in the car. "It didn't really want to go all the way back up the mountain."

"It's a couple of miles longer going up than going down," Mom said.

"Your mother used some of her Portuguese sweet bread for the French toast."

"Cool. I'm starting to get hungry," I said, then I sneezed one last really loud sneeze.

We talked a little on the way home. I can't remember what about, but I know that it felt so great for things to be normal again, at least for a while. I was going home for breakfast, and the sun was shining, and tomorrow I'd go back to school.

Then I wondered about something I hadn't thought of before. I wondered if I'd ever say anything to Sal about this.

No, I decided. Probably not. This business was between me and my mom and dad. We'd just keep going on one day at a time, like we were before. We'd probably find the birds and ask Ray or whoever was keeping them for him to give them back. But my neck prickled when I thought of seeing Ray again. Was I still scared of him?

By the time we got home, I decided that the answer to that was probably no, too. I didn't feel very afraid of him anymore. When I knew I couldn't hurt him when he was sleeping there, when it would've been easy for me to do, I'd stopped. But it wasn't because I was afraid of him.

Ray was wrong about Sal and me. We were brave.

* * *

Breakfast tasted so great, I couldn't believe it. My mom's Portuguese sweet bread was luscious just by itself, but when she made French toast with it, and served it with homemade guava syrup, oh, man! And with scrambled eggs and Portuguese sausage, well, that's what I'm gonna order for the first morning I get to heaven. And maybe half a papaya with lime squeezed on it. I wouldn't even need to look at the menu.

I could've sat there for an hour eating, but Mom reminded me that I had to get my school clothes on and my stuff together because Sal's mom was picking us up in fifteen minutes.

"Don't you have to check your eggs for the experiment?" she asked me later when I was heading toward the front door.

I hit myself on the forehead. "Yes! How could I forget the experiment? The scrambled eggs should've reminded me, at least."

Mom volunteered to do it, just this time only. Quick, before she changed her mind, I grabbed a notepad, wrote down what she needed to do, and gave her the clipboard for the measurements and things.

I thought for a minute about Honey Kealoha. She didn't have a mom now to do stuff for her like my mom did for me. I wondered if, when she got sad, she had anybody to talk with about things. Maybe her dad, and maybe Amy. She could talk to me, I guess. But we seemed to always be talking more about my problems than hers, and for a while she'd hardly talked to me at all. About anything.

Sal's mom pulled up the driveway and gave us two quick honks, so I had to finish thinking about Honey and give my mom a kiss on the cheek and scoot out the door. Em passed me and beat me to the car.

Before I loaded myself in next to Sal, I looked back at the house. My dad had come out on the lanai and he was watching us. He still had on his plaid flannel shirt, but it was tucked in his jeans and didn't look like a big nightgown now. He was standing up as straight and as tall as he could. I think that was the first time he ever waved to us when we took off for school. Or maybe it was the first time I ever looked back and noticed.

Sal high-fived me when I scooted in. Maybe things were normal again with us, I thought. We might never stop fighting about the rooster stuff, but I sure as heck wasn't going to say anything right then about our birds getting stolen.

But right when we started back down the driveway, Emily blurted it all out. "Somebody stole two of my daddy's best birds last night. They didn't even use the gate! They knocked part of the fence down flat. Isn't that terrible?"

"Oh, for heaven's sake!" Sal's mom said. "Your dad's beautiful roosters? Two, you say?"

Sal looked over at me while Emmie went on and on about the bird burglary. I finally stopped her by saying, "Well, we'll find them, I'm pretty sure, so let's just change the subject, okay?"

"Any idea who mighta snatched um?" Sal asked me, kinda quiet. When I didn't answer, he said, "Your dad needs to file a police report."

"Yeah. He'll probably do that." We were all quiet for a while then, even motormouth Emily. I remembered her joke about the old lady and said, "Hey, Em. Heard any good jokes lately?"

"Hey. Yeah! Allison Chang told me a new one. Why did the chicken cross the road?"

"No idea," Sal said, making a face at me.

"To prove he wasn't *chicken!* Funny, huh? And she told me this one, too...let me see. Oh, yeah. Why did the chicken cross the road?"

"I have no idea, Emily," Sal's mom said.

"Because it was Wednesday."

We all waited. Finally, Sal said, "And?"

"It was Wednesday, see, and he saw this sign on a restaurant across the road that said, 'Chicken: All you can eat on Wednesdays.' Get it? He thought it meant he could eat as much as he wanted to and..."

The three of us groaned all at the same time. I promised myself again that I just *had* to tell Emmie some better jokes.

TWENTY-ONE

I didn't see Raymond Salvador for a couple of weeks after the birdnapping, and that was okay with me. I worried that I might have more bad dreams about him—not the getting-dragged-into-his-van dreams, but worse nightmares where I'm standing over his bed and he wakes up and grabs my neck and strangles me or something. But I didn't see him, and I didn't dream about him even one time.

For two weeks, nothing much happened at all. Uncle Porky fixed the fence, and it looked as good as new when he got through. I overheard him talking with Dad about filing a police report, but Dad said no, he wouldn't do that.

At first I thought Dad had decided not to file a report because most of the police here aren't too happy with rooster people. The gambling and all. But later, I changed my mind.

Dad knew who would get arrested if he went to the police. He didn't see that little piece of yellow cloth stuck on the nail that awful morning like I did, but I'm sure he'd figured out who stole his birds. He didn't like or trust Ray, but the Salvadors were not just our neighbors. They were our friends.

Our moms were best friends, just like Sal and me. The Salvador family didn't need any more trouble than they already had. Especially not trouble from us.

It was a while before the subject of Ray even came up again after that. Then, on a Saturday morning, Emmie handed me the phone.

"Hello," I said.

"Paul. Hi," Sal said in his something's-going-on voice. "Listen...what're ya doing?"

"Um, nothing much."

"Come on over. You hafta help me with something."

"Sure. Whuzzup?"

"You'll see when you get here."

I said okay, but he'd already hung up. I told Dad where I was going, grabbed my slippers from off the porch, and headed over.

When I turned onto his driveway, I saw Sal in front of his carport, standing there with his arms folded. A rooster carrier was by him on the grass. He waved and pointed down at the cage, and when I got closer, I saw that there was another cage behind it. A soft noise came from the back cage.

I'd already guessed who was inside there. Then I saw them. "*Ho*...lee!" I said, looking over at Sal.

"Yeah. They're yours."

I bent down and looked into the Red's beady little eyes. "How'd you know? Where'd you get um?"

"Ray."

"You're kidding! He brought um back?"

"My dad brought um back, but Ray kinda said where we'd

find um." He shuffled his feet. "They had a little vacation over at Kenny Aguilar's."

"I knew...I mean, I *thought* Ray wouldn't take um home with him."

"You knew Ray had your birds?"

"Well, not for sure. My dad and me, we didn't wake up when he came. Just saw they were gone early in the morning."

Sal frowned. He rubbed the handle of one of the cages while he clued me in. "Well, I guess Ray and the guys got kinda drunk. They were arguing about how much this guy from Kauai would pay for those two birds. You remember—they were looking at um when they came to pick us up for the derby. So anyways, Ray said he'd go get the birds so they could find out and...well, you know what happened."

"Ray told you this?"

"Ray? Are you kidding? Nah. But he did tell Trini after a while. Not where he got um or where he was keeping um, but he told her he had a couple of birds that weren't really his. So when Trini saw my grampa at Pack 'n Pay, she asked him if he knew anybody who was missing a couple of roosters. She also said that Ray seemed to be feeling guilty about taking them. Go figure! My brother maybe getting a conscience or something?"

"Yeah, pretty weird." I made a face at the bird in the front cage. He tried to peck me through the mesh.

"Anyways," Sal said, "my grampa already suspected whose birds they were and when he found out where Ray took um, he called my dad. Kenny just handed um over to him a little while ago. He said it was okay with Ray. And that's all I know."

He lifted the front cage. "Here, grab this one. We'll take um the rest of the way home. Your dad'll be pretty happy to have um back, uh?"

"I can hardly wait to see his face!" I took the cage, Sal grabbed the other one, and we started down the driveway. We talked on our way back to my house, but he didn't say another word about his brother. I got the idea that he didn't want to talk about him anymore. But there was still one thing I needed to know. "Hey, Sal. I was just wondering. Why didn't your dad just drop these guys off at my house?"

He shrugged his shoulders. "I dunno. I wondered the same thing." We walked onto our driveway, then he said, "Maybe he's 'shame,' uh? Ray's grown up and doesn't live at home now, but my dad still feels responsible for him. For the stupid stuff he does. Probably he didn't want to hand these guys over to your dad in person any more than Ray did."

I nodded. "Well, at least Ray kinda gave um back, and they look okay."

"Sure. Ray's good with birds, you know."

My dad was in the infirmary over by the window when we slid the cages onto the big table that was next to our experiment incubator.

"What are you guys up to?" he asked us. We just grinned, so he grabbed his cane and came over to take a look at what we'd brought.

He looked from one cage to the other. I was right about how surprised and happy he'd be when he saw his birds. "Well, I'll be...," he said. "I can't believe you guys got them back! Where on earth? Where—?"

"Up at Kenny Aguilar's," I said. I was hoping he wouldn't ask how they got there, and he didn't. He just had this big grin when he looked at the Reds. "Well, I'll be…," he kept saying. Finally he grabbed his cane again and a pair of gloves. "How about coming along while I put these lost creatures back where they belong?"

We followed him into the rooster yard and put the cages down by their empty houses. Dad put the gloves on, reached in the carrying cages, and took out the first one. He attached it to its tether, then he looped the cord back over the stake. Next, he took out the other rooster and attached it to its tether. When he stood back up, he pulled his gloves off and stuck his hand out. "Thanks, Mr. Salvador," he said, shaking hands with Sal and nodding his head like a little bow. "And say 'mahalo' to your dad and anybody else who helped with this, okay?"

"Sure thing, Mr. Silva," Sal said. He looked away, like he was kinda embarrassed.

I think Dad felt that way, too, because he turned around and started back to the gate. When he got there, he said, "Now you guys go in and give your mom the good news. You should probably hit her up for some of that cake she just baked."

So after a few minutes me and Sal were all set up on the back lanai table, scarfing down *haupia* cake and cans of icy cold Pepsi. Sal took a noisy slurp out of his can and sat back on the bench with a sigh that turned into a super loud burp. "Oops! Sorry," he said, and we laughed. "Get no manners, das why, uh?"

When we stopped laughing, he looked down at his plate. I was busy eating the haupia layer off my cake. (Haupia's the coconut pudding that makes the cake taste so ono.) I heard him clear his throat.

"Um, Paulie. Maybe this is my conscience. Like Ray, uh? But that wasn't cool what I said about you and your dad being crazy. The rooster thing. I guess I was just surprised when you told me about the job and stuff. I really thought we felt the same. We hardly ever don't feel the same, right?"

"Yeah. I shoulda said something to you before that. Said how I really felt."

"Anyways, we can't think the same way about everything, can we?"

"I guess there's gotta be some things we don't agree on. Like what parts we like best in the samurai movies. We hardly ever like the same ones."

"And raw fish, maybe. You like regular sashimi, but not *poke.* Because of the sauce."

"Not the sauce. I don't like how the *limu* stirred in with the fish chunks smells and tastes. I'm not crazy about seaweed. But I can't think of very many other things we don't agree on."

Sal smiled and picked up his cake with his hands, eating the haupia off it the way I was doing. "Guess we'll be okay with the rooster stuff then," he said.

"Sure. No problem."

But it *had* been a problem. A huge problem, because ever since Sal said we were crazy and stomped out of my bedroom, a part of me had hurt whenever I thought about it.

And now it felt so good to know we were still friends. I would've felt even better if we both believed the same way, but being friends again was good enough for now.

"Anyways," Sal said after he wiped his fingers on his shirt and not on the cloth napkins Mom gave us, "I shoulda said this a while ago. Sorry, man."

"Me, too," I said. We high-fived over our cake plates.

It had been a really good morning. First the roosters coming back home. Then Sal. I licked the white crumbs off my plate. Sal picked his up and did the same thing, only he made a noise like a hungry dog slurping food out of his dish to make me laugh and I got Pepsi up my nose.

TWENTY-TWO

I had a good excuse for not thinking about the rooster problem for a while. I had tons of stuff to do, mostly homework. Two term papers—not long ones, but both were gonna be due this semester—and the science experiment, of course. Also the usual chores: helping my dad with things he couldn't do very well yet, and sometimes even helping my mom and watching Emily when they went someplace.

I also needed two new tires for my bike after my crazy ride down to Roger's house the other day. Guess I hit more potholes than I thought. Anyways, I had to spend some time after school making money to pay for the tires and some other stuff—mowing a few yards, helping old Mr. Freitas who lives a few blocks down the hill fix up his fence. The termites had eaten it bad, and we put on over thirty new boards and repainted the whole thing, so I made a few bucks there.

I was busy, but I couldn't forget my promises about the roosters. First the one I made to myself about not being a part of the fighting in any way, and then the one I made to help Dad find some different way of making money. I don't know why, but I'd thought the easiest promise would be the job one, and that when I'd found Dad a new job, that would take care of the other promise, and we'd all live happily ever after.

I know that sounds stupid, but I just was hopeful. Yeah, that's the word, *hopeful.* I'm not totally stupid about the real world. I knew that finding something for Dad wouldn't be as easy as finding work for myself. You can't support a family by painting fences and mowing acres of centipede grass for neighbors. But there *had* to be jobs for Dad. He just didn't know where to look, right?

I told myself that there wasn't any big rush on this and I tried to not think about it too much. But I did. Every morning when I'd go in front and look at our birds, I was reminded that we needed to make a change. They looked happy doing their bird things, but I'd started to picture them fighting each other. Pecking and stabbing, bleeding and dying—or even worse, winning and staying alive, but having to fight again.

Nothing much can be done for you if you're a rooster that's been bred and trained for the cockpit. You can't just retire from the ring, quit while you're ahead. You're not an ordinary bird who can just hang around a farm with the hens. You're a fighter, and no chickens are ever gonna be safe with you around. I don't know for sure if what Sal said was true about it being a fighting cock's nature to fight, to protect his territory. But whether it's his nature or just what people teach him, after a while, fighting is all he can do, just like the pit bulls that are trained to fight and can't be kids' pets anymore. It's sad, but what can you do?

The roosters were linked to fighting, and we couldn't be connected with the fighting anymore. So the only thing I could do was to find a way to get us out of this by getting job ideas together for my dad. I didn't have a deadline like you do for science projects and term papers, but every day I felt like I had to try, and I did. Plus I really worried about it a lot.

It got so I'd be at school and instead of listening to Mrs. Chong or Mr. Armstrong, I'd be thinking about new jobs. I'd come up with some job ideas I thought might work, but there were always problems with them when I thought about them some more.

I'd started reading the *Shoreline Tribune*'s want ads for jobs after everybody was through with the newspaper. A whole page of jobs was in there, but even I could tell that not one would be worthwhile for Dad.

"Accountant, Ace Carpets." Nah. Dad was good at keeping our books, but you need a license or something for a job like that. "Fry Cook, Paniola Pancake House." Not with Dad still hobbling around with a cane. Besides, that paid about as much as Mr. Freitas gave me for fixing fences. I didn't even read the ads for heavy equipment operators or longshoremen. No way could Dad do those, and most of the other ads were just as useless.

A couple of schools needed teachers, but Dad wasn't qualified, really, even though he was as smart as any teacher I ever had. Then I'd see something like "Fisherman for Trawler" and I'd think, hey, Dad's a great fisherman!

But that was before the accident.

I couldn't count the times I got all excited like that and

then disappointed. But after a few days of reading every tiny ad, I began to realize what Dad had meant. It wasn't a good job market right now, and he couldn't do a lot of the jobs that were out there. We wouldn't do roosters forever, but what was the alternative?

I stopped reading the ads when I finally noticed that the pages in that section of the newspaper had been folded over the other way, then folded back to normal. Dad had been going through that part of the paper every day, too.

I remembered that Junior Reeves said one time that his mom had a job she'd gotten on the Internet. I phoned him and he told me the site was something like "Job Search." You could look for jobs in the area where you lived.

I was pretty sure my dad hadn't checked the Internet yet, and I just knew I'd find the perfect job there. When Dad got some money after the accident, a settlement from the insurance company, he'd bought a computer for me. Once in a while I helped Dad look for something, but it was mine.

There were lots of jobs on the site. Like with the paper, I looked at each one, thinking "Yes!" a few times, then seeing it was on the other side of the island, or required a college degree, or was just something Dad couldn't do. I almost cried when I finished the last job on the list. "Writer, Advertising."

Man! Why had I been so sure I could do something that my dad couldn't do? I musta had "beeg head," like my friends say.

I didn't give up, though. I did a lot of other Web searches. Nothing. I talked to people, just kinda nosing around, but nobody knew anybody who needed help. Sal's dad checked out the hotel where he worked, but they weren't hiring. I just had to score *one* lousy job, that's all! So why couldn't I find it?

Then, all of a sudden, my mom said something that totally changed my whole world.

TWENTY-THREE

Mom had me helping her with a wreath project. We'd spread stuff out on the kitchen table, and I was using a hot-glue gun to attach dried woodroses to Styrofoam circles that she was turning into Hawaiian Christmas wreaths. I was unwinding some wire for her when she said, "Your dad is considering a job offer, Paul. Has he said anything to you?"

"What? A job offer? Mom, that's so cool!" I dropped the coil of wire and went over to her side of the table. "When did this happen? What job? Why hasn't he told me?"

"This just came up a couple of days ago—"

"A couple of *days*? You guys knew about this for a couple of days? For the whole weekend and you didn't say anything?"

Mom nodded, then she said in this ordinary voice, like she was trying to keep me from freaking out, "When we were at the hardware store, your dad got talking with your friend Eggie Fernandez's father. One of his workers at Mauna Kai Fresh Eggs is moving to the mainland, and he wondered if your dad was interested in applying."

"Man, that's so *cool!* We could still be in the chicken business, but we could phase out the roosters."

Mom gave me this long look. She didn't smile or anything. She just looked back down at her wreath. "Well, it's a possibility anyway."

"More than a possibility, Mom. I've been trying like crazy to figure this out, and here Dad has it all figured out without me even helping. Where is he? I've gotta talk with him."

"He's taking a short nap. Don't you wake him up, huh? He hasn't had a good night's sleep all this week. So just wait, okay? Talk with him after dinner, maybe."

I said okay, but Mom could tell from the mess I was making with the wire that my mind wasn't on woodroses, so she told me to go, scram. I piled the tangle of wire on the table and took off for my room.

I tried to work on my math, but I couldn't concentrate on that either, so I gave Sal a ring and told him about the job thing. Of course he wasn't all excited like me, but he said, "That's great, Paulie. I hope stuff works out for you guys."

I kept listening for Dad, hoping he'd come out of the bedroom. He'd told Mom about this, so why hadn't he said anything to me? Didn't he know how much I'd been worrying about this?

It seemed like it took an hour, but finally I heard Dad talking to Mom in the living room. In five seconds I was right there. When he said hi and that he was heading for the infirmary, I was out the door with him, walking along with him and asking him why he hadn't told me about the job.

"This is important to me, Dad," I said when he turned on the infirmary lights. "You're gonna take the job, right?"

"I'm not sure at this point," he said. "But you're right. You have a vested interest in this, too, Paul. And maybe you can help me think this through." He started scooping chicken feed out of a 40-pound bag into a small bucket. "So just how much did your mother tell you?"

"That Eggie's dad needs help at Mauna Kai." Dad kept on scooping. "Don't you see? That's perfect! You know everything there is to know about eggs, and chickens, too. So what's to decide?"

Dad put the half-filled bucket on the floor and sat down on one of the stools. "Sit," he told me. "We need to discuss this."

I pulled another stool over to the table and sat across from him, folding my hands like if I was at some kind of business meeting. "Okay then," I said. "What's the job like?"

"Well, it doesn't really involve the chickens or the eggs much, so my world-famous talents with the creatures would be wasted." We both smiled, and he said, "Matt Fernandez offered me the position of night manager at the plant."

"So you have, like, first dibs on the job? It sounds cool."

"The title sounded okay to me, too, but the job description left a little to be desired. I'd have a couple of things to do with the hens, but from what Matt says, I'd be more a night watchman than a manager. I'd take over from the day manager around seven, then work a twelve-hour shift."

I was calming down a little. "Well, at least things would probably be pretty quiet. You'd be your own man, right? You could maybe take some university courses, like you talked about a long time ago? Be a teacher, maybe. You'd be a good teacher."

"I thought about that. Yeah, I'd have plenty of time on my hands. I wouldn't see much of you kids because I'd be asleep most of the time when you were home. But you and Em would probably like that, right?"

"Sure," I said, pretending I was serious. "That would be the best part."

"And the work wouldn't involve much physical labor. Nothing to the job that I couldn't handle, even the way I am now. I'd have a radio to use if there was a problem. An alarm system."

"Hey, you could do your therapy while you were working, too. To keep awake. How cool is that?"

Dad gave a little laugh. But just a *really* little one. Then we were back to our business meeting again.

"Paul, if I do take the job, there will be some changes I'd have to make…and just about as many for you and your mom and Emily. The salary Matt could offer is pretty much minimum wage. There's just no way we could stay here, keep up the mortgage…"

He said some more stuff about equity in the house and something else, but I was still trying to get ahold of what this would mean. Finally I said, "Wait. We'd have to move? We couldn't stay here?"

"Your mom and I've been going through the figures, Paul, and, yes, that's what we'd need to do."

"But where…?"

"Well, we've been working on that, too. The Terrace Condominiums are pretty affordable. You know—those new ones being built near the mall downtown? Well, they're in a good location, and they're selling the first units for reasonable prices. We could sell the house here, and our fee-simple acreage, and get enough money so a mortgage wouldn't be a problem anymore."

"But a *condo*," I said. "A stupid, tiny little condo? Dad, you can't be thinking about this. Seriously! You'd give up this house, the trees, the...the *freedom* we have here just so you could take a job you could probably do in your sleep?"

"That was my first thought, too, son. Your mom started crying and—"

"That's what I feel like doing right now, too. And wait...what's gonna happen to Milo?"

Dad settled himself more on the middle of his stool. "We checked into that yesterday. Got blueprints, house rules, and everything. No pets except for birds. And of course Em could bring her guppies. You'd both have a room of your own there, like here. Just smaller, of course."

I got up off my stool and kicked at it with my toe until it was back under the table. I'd heard enough. My parents had gone crazy. "Well," I said. "You'll just have to tell Mr. Fernandez no way! You wanted me in on this decision and that's what I've decided. When do you have to let him know?"

"I have 'first dibs' on the job, as you put it, but just until next Sunday. If I don't take it, he'll place an ad in the *Shoreline* on Monday. With the job market as lousy as it is now, somebody will probably pounce right on it, as you've probably guessed—"

"Yeah. I've been reading the paper after you."

"I know, son. We've both done a lot of soul-searching on this, haven't we?"

"Yes." I said. I leaned over and rested my arms on the table. Put my forehead down on them for a minute to calm down. "I'm sorry. I shouldn't be thinking just about me," I mumbled, then I straightened back up. "You and mom—you love living here as much as I do. Mom would never have a garden like now, and we wouldn't ever have next-door neighbors like the Salvadors. And if I hadn't kept reminding you about the roosters, well…"

"No. We needed that reminder," Dad said. "Don't be sorry about that."

"But this is so much change, Dad! You know how I feel about Milo. He's part of our family. Even Emily will miss him. This doesn't seem fair."

I was glad Dad didn't answer and didn't remind me of all the things that aren't fair in this life. He just scooted his stool back. It made a woody kind of squeak on the cement floor. He grabbed his cane from where it was hooked over the edge of the table.

"It's about time for dinner, I'm guessing," he said. "Just think about all of this, okay? We still have almost a week to figure out what's best for all of us."

I promised him I would. And I knew that I wouldn't think of anything else for a single minute until he called Eggie's dad and gave him the news. I wouldn't say anything to Emmie, I told him. This was between him, Mom, and me. Em was too young to understand this kind of stuff.

* * *

I closed the infirmary door behind me while Dad finished up inside. I took a couple of steps up to the house, but then I stopped. I didn't know why. Maybe it was because the house—the whole world, really—had changed colors since I went outside.

The sun was low and the sky was getting pink, turning everything else pink and orange. Up here, we can see sunrises, but not sunsets—the sun going into the ocean. But that doesn't mean we don't have this huge sky changing colors every night. I looked above our house at our forest of ohia and tree ferns and bamboo. A shama thrush was singing to somebody back in the bamboo. Our house looked small where it was in all of the trees, low, with a shake roof, and it was just right for where we were—it was Hawaiian feeling. Warm feeling.

The Terrace Condos were nice, like Dad said. Very modern. Built around a courtyard with places where you could barbecue. Sal and me had been keeping an eye on the construction. It was fun. But we also felt bad when we remembered what had been there before—four big old homes where families lived for years. One-story Hawaiian-style houses like ours, only bigger, and they fit in where they were between the black rock walls all splattered with bright green moss and whitish lichen. They were gone now. Even the rock walls had been knocked down.

Dad came out and locked the infirmary door. He walked up the driveway and looked at me to see if I'd follow him, but

I didn't. So he climbed the steps to the lanai, holding onto the railing with one hand and his cane with the other. It took him way more than a year to be able to go up steps that way, or down steps, even. Dad was a fighter, like Grampa Alberto's best roosters. I knew he'd be fine some day.

I turned around and looked at the clouds. We almost always have clouds to watch here on the hills. Lots are gray and bring rain, but not these. Their bottom silver edges were turning gold, and the middles were getting rose and orange. Some were even purple.

I picked up a long, dried-up palm frond and walked up the length of our fence, dragging the branch along the chain links. They were still vibrating when I got to the gate, where I dropped the branch.

I turned back around when I got to the lanai and looked over the railing down to the bay. The hotel people were turning their lights on. So was a huge cruise ship that was moored in the bay for the night. I was too high up to see any little fishing boats, but I knew that they were pulling into the piers. Their catches would be put on huge piles of ice for the fish auction really early tomorrow morning.

Milo came up from the lawn. He didn't walk straight over to me. He kind of zigzagged so when he finally rubbed my leg with one long swoop, he acted like he just happened to end up there, and not that he liked me or anything. He was so cool.

I looked at our soft, thick grass, then at Milo, and I started feeling better again. We couldn't leave. We couldn't just give him away. I took a big breath of cool air and noticed that the mock orange blossoms were popping out on the hedge. That was the nice smell I'd noticed when I came outside.

Then rooster #43 piped up, reminding me that he was there on the other side of the fence. I wouldn't look at him. He was safe, anyway. Uncle Porky said he'd make a lousy fighter, and my dad said we could just keep him if I wanted to. But I looked at the other birds and decided that I didn't really love the roosters anymore.

This was all their fault. Without them, I wouldn't have to deal with all the cockfighting business and the making-a-living business. Why should I have to choose between helping them and leaving the only place where I would ever be happy? Well, too bad, roosters. You can just take care of yourselves.

I turned around again and went inside. Dad was talking to Mom in the front room. Her eyes looked funny, kinda swollen. This must not be much fun for her, either, I thought.

Emmie would cry for months if we had to leave. I decided she didn't ever need to know how close we came to moving and leaving old Milo.

We all went in the kitchen and Mom scooped some good stew into our bowls, but Emily was the only one who ate very much dinner.

TWENTY-FOUR

I still had my outline for my English paper to do, so I skipped dessert and went to my room. Every time I'd start to work on it, though, a stupid rooster would crow and remind me of everything else. I finally took a shower and just sat there on my bed. Milo came in, but I got up and nudged him back out with my bare foot.

For a second, I felt like it would be good to talk with somebody like Honey about all of this. But I'd tried a couple of times since I told her about the cockfight, and so far she didn't want to talk. I wasn't sure why, exactly.

Should I phone Sal? No. That wouldn't be any better. I already knew how *he* felt about all of this.

Why, I wondered, didn't I have Sal's dad instead of mine? He was a normal kind of dad, and there was no way he'd ask Sal or Ray or even Mrs. Salvador to help him make a decision. Ever. He'd decide something, and they'd do it.

So why did I have to get a dad who thought *I'd* know what we were supposed to do with our lives? I'm a kid. When I'm old and married, I'll have to decide stuff like this, but not now. And when I'm the father, I'm going to be like Mr. Salvador. What I say goes. That's how things should be.

I plunked down on my bed and thought about when I'd told Dad that we'd just have to get out of the cockfighting business. Sal's dad would have laughed his head off if Sal had done that. Well, I guess I've learned something. Don't tell adults what they should do. Especially if you aren't ready to hang on and see what might happen.

The trade winds started blowing my curtains straight into the room. It was getting cold, so I got up and closed the wooden louvers. At the Terrace Condos they had just a few little windows. They didn't need louvers because everything was air-conditioned—new and clean and nice. But every time I thought about moving, my throat felt all tight clear down to my chest.

I remembered telling Dad that me and Em could go to a different school to save money. I'd do it, too, if it would help. But not give up this house. Not these hills, the pond up above us, and all the great memories I have here.

There's no way I'm leaving now.

Don't think about the cockfights again, I told myself. There are some things you can't help, and the roosters are one of those. If they end up in cockfights, that's just what they're supposed to do. Like Sal said, that's their nature. And something else—when I made my big decision, I'd just watched a bloody, terrible fight. I was sick and all upset. You don't think very well when you're like that.

I turned off the lamp and crawled under my quilt. I watched the red numbers on my clock radio change, one slow minute after another until finally my bird alarm clock started crowing. My squawky bird who was safe and wouldn't ever know what gaffs were for.

Another rooster with a lower voice started in then, and two with crows that sounded almost like yodels joined in. One by one the roosters told me it was a new morning, and right then I knew what I had to do.

* * *

"Morning, Paul," Dad said when I went in the kitchen. He looked me over, from my crazy hair on down. "Wow," he said. "You look dreadful!"

"Worse than usual?" I tried to smooth my hair down, but it was all wild from me getting twisted and untwisted in the quilt all night.

"Yup. You're even more of a mess than you usually are when you stagger out here in the mornings." He smiled and closed the newspaper.

I couldn't see what section he'd been looking at. Maybe the want ads. But it didn't make any difference. I had to tell him.

"I didn't sleep very much," I said. "But I know what we have to do now. We have to stop helping the cockfighters hurt and kill the roosters."

Dad locked his fingers together and looked at me. "You mean that, Paul? Even if we have to move?"

"Yeah. Even if we hafta move. It'll be okay with me."

Quick, I turned around so he couldn't see my face and

went back in the bathroom. I ran cold water and splashed it on my cheeks, then I brushed my hair so hard every hair hurt.

TWENTY-FIVE

It was still early, so I took my time getting dressed. I even made my bed all nice with the quilt's big green breadfruit pattern exactly in the middle. Before I went to the kitchen to have some cereal, I picked my sweater up off the floor and hung it in its place in the closet.

Later I dragged the science project out of my room, and that made things look even neater. This was the day our projects were due.

Mrs. Salvador picked us up in their SUV, and Mom got in the front seat with her. She was going with Mrs. S. to get groceries and stuff after they dropped us off.

Mrs. S. pulled into our school's half-circle driveway. Sal grabbed both of our backpacks, and I carried our science project, which was big and awkward but not too heavy. I said 'bye to Em, and Sal and me turned the other way to go to Mrs. Chong's homeroom.

"Need help with that thing?" Sal asked.

"Nah," I said. "I've got it. Just get the door, okay?" We went inside Mrs. Chong's room and I leaned our project up by the side blackboard. "What do you think our chances are with this, Sal?"

"Hey, we've got the thing aced, man! Nothing but A's for this baby."

I looked over our display. We'd put a lot of work in it and it showed. We'd finally finished it, and I'd been so stoked about how it had turned out.

But now, it just seemed okay. I was having problems getting excited about anything now. I'd start to feel good about the project, or getting out of the rooster business, or Dad making a new start with work...then I'd picture us packing up everything—everything except Milo—and backing down our driveway for the last time, headed away from home and down to our small condo near the mall.

But I knew that Sal was right when he said we'd get a good grade on the project. Our project proved what our theory had said—the humidity in the incubator had an effect on the hatchability of the eggs. More strong, perfect chicks hatched from the eggs that were kept at the middle humidity. We'd tested three different conditions, and the 75 percent humidity worked best.

I'd typed stuff up on the computer and used a big, cool-looking font on the folding display boards Sal had designed. Then, in the same font, but in huge letters, I made the sign for the top: "THE EFFECTS OF HUMIDITY UPON THE HATCHABILITY OF EGGS." It looked great. And I'd put everything through spell-check so Mrs. Chong wouldn't have a fit if I spelled *hatchability* wrong in giant letters.

"*Effects* or *Affects*?" Sal had asked me when he'd glued up the sign. He stood back a ways to look at it.

"*Effects.* Geez, Sal. Good thing I did the writing part of the experiment."

"Yeah, yeah. But you gotta admit, this thing is artistic, right? If you'd done the design part, it would've been messy and outta balance and—"

"I know, I know. And we never would've finished. But look at this. We're done!"

"Yeah, we're pau. Way to go, partner! Woooo hah!" He hit me on the back. I pounded him back.

Mrs. Chong came over to have a look at our project. We watched her face when I opened up the panels. She squinted at the small printing for a minute. Then she said, "I have to admit it, Mr. Salvador and Mr. Silva. At first glance, at least, it looks really good. I'm quite impressed."

Sal and me gave a silent "Yeah!" and we high-fived behind her back. For Mrs. Chong, "impressed" was good. Really good.

Honey and Amy came in then and set up their display by the windows. It looked pretty good, too, so I went over to check it out.

"How does it look?" Honey asked me.

"Looks good," I said. "I'm…uh…impressed."

"Thank you," she said. "And hey, Paul…do you want to eat lunch together tomorrow? I'll pack a couple of sandwiches and some other stuff. If it's still nice like this, we could eat under the banyan and talk for a while."

This surprised the heck out of me. I'd been trying to find a way to get talking again, and here she talked to me first. "Sure," I said. "That'll be okay. They probably have the Friday Fish Surprise at the caf, but I can try to live without that for one week. Wait a minute…what kind of sandwiches?"

"Probably just peanut butter and jelly, but the jelly's really good. Poha berry my dad picked up at the farmers' market." She smiled. "And I have Portuguese sweet bread, like you like. You can get us drinks from the machine, okay?"

I smoothed my hair down, tried to be cool. "Okay. How about chips?"

"I'll pack chips."

"Okay. See ya at the banyan…tomorrow." I started to walk away, still not believing we were gonna do this. Then I stopped and said, "Twelve-thirty?"

"Yeah, about twelve-thirty."

"Okay. Thanks, uh?"

Well, at least I had one thing to look forward to in my life.

I went back over to Sal just when Mrs. Chong was showing Eggie Fernandez and Matt Kamalama where to put their project. "Bet Mrs. C. won't be very impressed with that one," I told Sal. "It looks kinda junk, if you ask me." Mrs. C. took her time, though, and read through all their stuff.

Last week Mrs. C. had promised she'd give us our grades today after her free period. And one thing about Mrs. Chong—she always kept her promises to us. Also, she knew we couldn't take very much suspense on this. It was a big hunk of our science grade and we'd go pupule if we had to wait until Monday. So right before lunch she gave Sal and me the signal for our conference.

"Paul. Sal," Mrs. C. said. "I believe that both of you have the capacity to do something big. Something creative and worthwhile. I'm giving you a well-deserved A on your incubation experiment, but next year, I expect you to challenge yourselves even more than you did this time. Next year, you'll be working individually, and the kids with the best projects will travel to Oahu for the regional competitions. You'll need greater scope to your projects to get that far."

I said, "Sure, Mrs. Chong."

Sal said, "You probably won't be our science teacher next year, right?"

She laughed. "Right. You might have Mr. Miyagi. He's just been hired, so they'll probably give him the kids who are the most trouble."

"That's us," Sal said, grinning at me.

"But I still expect you to remember what I want from you. I'll still be around, God willing, and I'll make sure Mr. Miyagi doesn't let you just goof off."

With our conference and our science project over, I had to find something else to think about besides moving to the condo, so I let my mind think about lunch with Honey. I was pretty sure that she wasn't mad at me, or she wouldn't have wanted to eat lunch with me at all. Instead, she wanted to meet at the banyan. But I still was wondering what was going on with her when we loaded up the station wagon after school and Sal told everybody about how we'd aced our project, royally.

TWENTY-SIX

Our school's campus has tons of trees. Luckily for me, no mangos, but plenty of allspice trees, with their red and gold leaves mixed in with the green ones so they look kinda like pictures of mainland trees in the fall. The three big royal poinciana trees in front of the classroom building had already lost their red flowers and looked like they had big, green, lacy-looking fans on them now.

But we had only one banyan tree, in back of the tennis courts, and it was a giant. Long, ropy roots hung down from almost every branch. The little kids used to swing on them like Tarzan until the principal put the tree off-limits for swinging. Not because the kids would get hurt, he said, but because it wasn't good for the tree.

No kids, big or little, were by the banyan when I walked out. Just Honey, who was sitting there in her blue T-shirt and her yellow skirt. I had to keep myself from having a silly grin when I went over and sat down by her on the old bench. "Ya don't think we'll get ants here?" I asked.

"I haven't seen any yet, and I've had these out for a couple of minutes." She pointed to two nice fat sandwiches sitting there on a blue cloth.

"I just got these," I said, plunking two cans of juice down on the bench. "I think they're phasing out the sodas. Nothing in there except 7-Up, but I got us one guava juice and one POG. Take your pick."

She pointed to the passionfruit-orange-guava drink and I opened it for her. She said thanks and pulled her sandwich's plastic wrap open with her pink-painted fingernails. She took a little bite, then she got right down to business.

"Paulie. I'm sorry."

"Um. For what?"

"For not really talking to you much since you told me about the cockfight."

"Yeah. I guess I shouldn't have ruined your appetite that day, huh? You looked mad."

She took a sip of her juice, then she shook her head and put the can down. "No. I'm sorry I made you think that. I wasn't mad at all. Maybe I was kinda disappointed."

"With me?"

She thought about that for a second. "I guess so. You were trying to show me that you didn't enjoy the fighting. But…all I heard was this whole long story about eyes getting gouged and food booths and Ray being nice to his brother and stuff. You seemed so excited about everything."

I tried to remember what I'd said that day. She was wrong about me liking the cockfight, but I guess that was my fault. I guessed I was trying to be macho. I didn't tell her about getting sick, that's for sure.

I licked off some poha jelly that was dripping from my sandwich. "Really," I told her, "I felt pretty awful. I tried to tell you that, but I didn't know how, I guess."

"No, you did. You said you hated the fighting so much you wanted your dad to stop it, but it sounded to me like just *talk*, Paul. Like you were saying it because you thought that was what I wanted to hear."

"Maybe some of it was, right then. Just talk. I was stupid, thinking I could just tell Dad, 'That's it, no more raising roosters.' We'd sell them and everything would be fine forever."

"The thing is, Paulie, I should've remembered you're not like that. We've known each other forever, huh?"

I let out a deep breath. Then I drained my guava juice and put my sandwich down on my lap. "Since small-kid-time, for sure," I said.

Then I told her everything that had happened since I talked to her that day. It felt good to tell her. She was quiet until I got to the part about having to move to the Terrace Condos.

"I can't picture you or your family in one of those condominiums," she said. "When you showed me around your farm, I could tell how much you loved it."

"My whole family loves it there," I admitted. "This is going to be pretty hard."

"I wish there was something else you could do." She looked at me with a question in her eyes, but I just shook my head.

Then I said, "Everything will be okay. We can do it."

She reached out for a thin, stringy banyan root that was hanging down beside her. She wrapped it around and around her wrist and stared at it for a minute.

"I have to believe you," she said. "Everything will work out. And I know what you're doing is right, but..." She looked up at me. "Do the condos allow pets? What about Milo?"

Her face looked so worried, I couldn't just tell her no, Milo wasn't allowed. "We're not really sure on that yet," I told her. "We'll be okay."

"They *don't* take pets, do they? You'll have to leave him."

So much for keeping the truth from Honey. "I'll find somebody to take him," I said.

"*I'll* take him," she said without waiting even one second. "I've only seen him one time but I think he liked me."

"Then that settles one more thing. See? Everything will be fine."

We were through eating by then, and it was getting close to time to go back inside, so we tossed stuff in the bag she'd brought the sandwiches in and I dumped everything in the rubbish bin by the tennis courts. She folded up the blue cloth and tucked it in her backpack.

"So, thanks for lunch," I said when we were almost all the way back.

"Oh…yeah. Thanks for the drinks. We'll do this again sometime. Wait. I have an idea. Why don't I come over to your house? Maybe…on Sunday?"

"Sunday? Yeah. Sure. That would be good."

"We can talk, if you want—or not."

That was when I knew she was thinking the same thing I was. Sunday was going to be hard. It was the deadline with Mr. Fernandez. Then we'd know for sure which way my family was headed.

I looked at her face. She smiled, but I could tell that she was having almost as hard a time at being cheerful as I was, and I liked her even more than before. "You can come over anytime," I said. "Well…anytime after church. Wanna eat lunch at our house?"

"My dad likes to stop at the farmers' market downtown on Sundays. Then we have lunch at the little place across from there…"

"The organic one that has food that's healthy but still tastes good," I said.

"Yeah. Sunny's. That's where we always went with my mom." She walked a couple of steps, then she said, "But I could probably come over for lunch if you want."

"Nah. After lunch is fine."

"Okay. It'll probably be around one, one-thirty. I'm sure Dad can drop me off. Won't you be glad when we can just *drive?*"

"Yeah. Having to get somebody to take you everywhere you can't get to on your stupid bike, or just walk to, or take the bus to—that's a huge hassle."

"Uh-huh. So…Sunday…and I'll see you at school before that, of course."

"Oh, yeah, of course. See ya," I said, and we pushed the doors open and walked out of the fresh air into the crowded hallway that smelled like school.

TWENTY-SEVEN

After school that day, my mom dropped me off at the mall so I could do some shopping. I decided I had plenty of time, so I stopped at Trini Mendoza's surf shop. The bells on the door jingled when I went in.

"Paulie!" Trini said when she turned around. "I haven't seen you for *ages!*"

I went over and she gave me a big hug. She smelled like oranges. Not like orange soap or perfume or something. Like real oranges.

"Oops," she said. "Did I get juice on your shirt? I was just eating one of these terrific oranges. Raymond brought them back from his friend Eddie's. Eddie's folks have this great orchard up the mountain a ways. Hey. Where's your partner in crime? Sal didn't come with you?"

"Nope. He thinks he's getting a sore throat."

"Ah, too bad. But if he's like his brother, he'll be fine. Raymond's always sure he's coming down with something. And not just a cold. If he reads about malaria or, um, asbestos poisoning, anything like that, he's got it. He's such a big baby!"

Trini went back to the counter and pulled a huge orange off the top of a heap of oranges she had in a basket there and tossed it to me. "Raymond picked I don't know how many bags full. Maybe twenty. I'll give you a bag when you leave." She picked up the orange she'd already peeled and took a bite. "Mmmm," she said, her eyes almost closed. "Aren't these the most delicious things in the world? Local oranges are ugly, but they're the best. Eat. I've got hand wipes for after."

Okay. I should've expected that Trini would mention Raymond, but three or four times already in about three minutes? I'd have been happy if nobody ever said his name again, ever, but it looked like I was going to have to get used to it. To Trini, he was just a regular person. A regular boyfriend.

I wasn't too happy about eating anything Raymond Salvador had touched, either, but I peeled my orange. Pretty soon I was as messy as Trini, who was facing me from behind the shop's long counter.

"So," she said. "What brings you down the hill this afternoon?"

"My mom dropped me off after school so I could buy some stuff. I've got to go to Shiro's Bike Shop and pick up bike tires first. Mine are both wasted."

"Yeah. They don't last forever. Mine don't, that's for sure, riding here every day." She looked over at her racing bike, which was parked by the side wall. All along that wall were surfboards with every color and design. Above them, three shelves were loaded with skegs and leashes and everything.

An aluminum ladder was propped against the shelves. I guess Trini needed it to reach all the stuff, because she wasn't more than an inch taller than me. She was little and cute, with sparkly black eyes and really short hair. I thought for a second I might tell her about how I wrecked my bike tires riding down to Roger's house, but that thought didn't last long. No way would I tell anybody about that morning.

Trini said to help myself to another orange when I'd fnished, and I grabbed a big one from the basket, and was slurping up its juices while I looked around again. It was so ono.

"Were those here when me and Sal came here last time?" I asked, noticing that the whole back wall behind Trini was covered with paintings. I looked up at one of a monster wave with a tiny surfer in its curl, a really gnarly wave that looked like it would swallow the surfer kid the very next second.

"Uh-uh. Just the boards and surf paraphernalia, and all the T-shirts and stuff over on that side. I added the photos and paintings a couple of months ago. I'm close to the mall and hotels and I'm starting to get tourists from the ships walking over now, so I've become a little art gallery here. It's working out great, and the local artists love it."

Trini handed me a couple of hand wipes, then said, "Pretty soon that bunch of condos on the other side of the mall are going to have people moving in, and that might help business, too."

I gulped down my last bite of orange and smiled, but I wished she hadn't mentioned the condos. Today had been okay, with school getting my mind off things a little, and it seemed like Trini's shop and the mall were perfect places to...well, to hide for a while. It felt good being where nobody knew what was going on at our house.

"Nice pictures," I said. "I like that one best, I think." I pointed to the gnarly wave one. When I did, a shadow crossed the picture wall, and even if I hadn't heard the bells jingle on Trini's door I'd have known that somebody had come in the shop.

Trini looked up. Her eyes kinda crinkled at the corners first, then her mouth curved into this big, really happy smile. I looked over my shoulder, and there was Raymond Salvador, blocking the light.

Well, I decided, Trini's shop wasn't a very good place for hiding from anything or any*body*.

Ray walked over and plunked a huge gunnysack of oranges down on the floor beside the counter. His hair was lots shorter and he had on a new-looking blue aloha shirt.

"Who's your new boyfriend?" he asked Trini.

"Cute guy, huh?" she said, and she reached across the counter and messed up my hair. "I love this guy's hair," she said. "It has personality. It has character! Not like yours, Raymond. Yours is so...ordinary."

I felt my face blushing, but Trini and Ray were just looking at each other, not at me, and he was smiling at her just the way she smiled when she saw him. They wouldn't have noticed if I was blushing as red as a poha berry.

"Hey," Ray said to her, "at least I got this 'ordinary' hair chopped off for you. Whaddya want, girl?" He turned to me then. "Sal not here with you, Paul? I thought you guys were

Siamese twins. Never went anywhere without each other."

Trini answered for me. "Your brother has a sore throat, but I'm glad my boyfriend Paulie's here. I've missed him. Think we have enough oranges to spare a couple of small bags? He could take one up the hill to your folks, too."

"Really small-kine bags, maybe," Ray said. "That's all." He wasn't looking at me then, and I tried not to look at him. I felt like grabbing a few oranges and getting out of there as fast as I could run, but then Ray surprised me.

"I'll get bags for you, Paul," he said. "And Trini, where'd you put the shirts I pulled out for Sal and Paul? The black T-shirts with the 'Who da Surfah?' logos? You know, the ones from that promotional batch the A2Z people gave you last month."

"Oh, yeah! I'd have forgotten if you hadn't said something. Just a sec." She went into the little storage room by the swimsuit racks. "I hid them somewhere in here." I heard her rummaging around, then she said, "Yeah! Found um."

She came out and handed Ray the shirts. He unfolded one and held it up to me. "Perfect," he said. "Told you these would fit the kids, Trini. Here, Paul. You can take um up with the oranges."

"Thanks, uh?" I said. "These are pretty cool. Sal will like um, too."

I was still in shock. Ray Salvador was acting like a regular person. He was talking regular English to Trini and not pidgin. I didn't even know he could do that! But even weirder was that he was being thoughtful. And kind of nice.

Was he really getting a conscience, like Sal said? Or was he planning to pull some really nasty trick on me, waiting until I started to trust him?

Oh, no, Raymond Salvador, I said to myself. You're just being nice because of Trini. It's gonna take lots more than oranges and T-shirts to make me unsuspicious.

"Wait a second," Trini said, looking at me. "After you get your bike tires and other stuff, and oranges for you and the Salvadors, that's going to be a lot to handle. How are you getting home? Your mom's picking you up, right?"

"She can't. I'm taking the bus back."

"Whoa," Ray said. "You can't pack all that stuff to the bus, if one even comes on time, which it hardly ever does, and then carry everything up the driveways." He thought for a few seconds, then asked, "Can you shop, then be back here at six-fifteen? No later? I'll give you a ride. I've got some stuff to do now, but I'll come back when Trini closes up."

"Thanks," I said again. "Uh...I think I can do the bus thing, though. Two little bags of oranges won't be heavy."

Trini and Ray both started laughing. "Paulie, honey," Trini said when they stopped, "Raymond was just teasing you. There are no small bags—they're huge. He's going to load you up with more oranges than you could ever carry to the bus stop. Right, Raymond?"

"Sure thing. So ya better take my offer." He put his hand on Trini's shoulder, gave her a quick little kiss on the cheek, which of course I didn't watch, and headed for the door. "That's six-fifteen, kid. I'm heading to work after I drop you off."

"Yeah, sure. Thanks. See ya at six-fifteen."

Ray gave Trini a little salute and left, and I was just going to ask her about what kind of work Ray had got when the doorbells jingled again and three guys came in. The two younger dudes headed straight for the surfboards. The older guy wearing a tucked-in aloha shirt and a straw hat stopped by the windows and folded his arms, looking around at the whole shop. Trini said "Aloha, gentlemen" to them, and I gave her a wave and headed out to get my new tires. I was still wondering what would happen when I got back.

TWENTY-EIGHT

Shiro Watanabe gave me a good price on the bike tires. He told me to wait a sec while he looked in back, and he came right out with a good used tire I could keep for a spare. "Fo free, kid," he said, winking at me. Shiro's a nice old guy.

It didn't take long to buy some new rubber slippers at the mall and the felt-tip pens I needed for school. I got back to Trini's a couple of minutes after six.

"Hey there," Trini said when she heard her doorbells and saw who came in. "You've brought me good luck, Paul."

"Luck?"

"When you were leaving, you saw the man in the straw hat with the red-and-yellow feather lei around it?"

I nodded.

"He bought your big wave painting up there. Paid cash. I'll pack it up and have Raymond deliver it to his hotel tomorrow. Even better—the man showed me his website, which is really awesome, and he's sending a photographer to take digital shots of those abstracts." She pointed at three small square paintings, all in blue and green and foamy-looking white.

"So see? You're a lucky charm for me. And I'm a lucky lady. Got myself a little business I love here that pays my bills, a guy, and hey! Lucky we live Hawaii, huh?"

"Um, yeah. Lucky. All that stuff. That's great."

Trini started smiling when she saw my face. "Paulie, you're having trouble with my list of blessings, aren't you?" I looked down, and she said, "My guy is Raymond Salvador. You knew that, didn't you?"

"Oh. Sure." I kept my head down. "Sal said." I decided to look at her, then, and to be honest. "I think Raymond's lucky, but I mean…it *sounds* kind of like he's changed, right, but isn't he still the same old Raymond?"

Trini's face was all serious. "You're right, honey. He's not changed. He'll always be himself. He's not *changed*, but he's *changing*. Really changing, little by little."

"Because of you, right?"

She looked out the windows and shook her head. "Don't I *wish!*"

I was kinda proud that Trini was talking with me about grown-up things. But it was embarrassing, too, especially talking about Raymond, so I didn't say anything else.

"Paul, if I ever once thought that I could put Raymond Salvador on a better path, all by myself, I gave that up years ago. I broke up with that guy so many times…well, probably a hundred!"

"But nobody can change somebody else," I said, real quiet.

Trini looked at me in a funny way, like my mom looks at

my dad sometimes when she says something I don't understand but he does. "You're wise beyond your years. If hoping and trying and even praying could have done it, Raymond Salvador would be Father Damien by now!"

She made her hands like she was praying and laughed. "I finally gave up," she said. "Ray wanted to move in with me when his dad made him leave, and I said no. It was the best thing I ever did."

"So he started changing by himself then?"

She took a while and then she said, "Maybe. I didn't see him for a while. But something usually triggers real changes, you know what I mean?" I nodded. "Well, from what Raymond told me last month, when we started talking again"—she took a deep breath—"he'd been thinking a lot, and what started it had something to do with a rock. A black lava rock. Isn't that the weirdest thing you ever heard?"

I'd started tuning out some of the talk, but I sure paid attention then. Had Ray been thinking about the rock I left by his stupid head that morning at Roger's?

"A black rock? What did he say?"

She shook her head. "Very little, really. Just there was this rock, and that somebody could've killed him with it."

"But what happened with it?" I corrected myself. "I mean, where was it? What was the deal with it?"

"I don't know any more than that. But someone certainly put the fear of God in him."

Then Trini said, "And I know Raymond will be happy to tell you about his new job. You can ask him about it when he drives you home."

I nodded. At least I'd have one thing to say when we were alone with each other.

Trini went into her storeroom-office and came out with a big cardboard carton.

"Here," she said. She dropped it on the floor by my feet. "For your stuff. This'll be heavy when we get all the oranges in it, but Raymond can carry it."

Just as she finished her sentence, the bells on the door jingled and Ray came in. "Raymond can do what?" he asked.

"Carry this when it's all filled up. Paul, you can put your tires and things over here on the bottom. I put two empty bags inside for the oranges, and here are the T-shirts."

Raymond shook his head. "See how bossy she is, Paul?"

"Yeah," I said, "but she's a girl, right?"

"Go home, Paul. Just get out of here," Trini told me, but she was smiling. We put the oranges in and said goodbye, then Ray tossed the box in the back of his van like it had a couple of pillows in it, not a ton of oranges and my other stuff. He unlocked my door and went around to the driver's side.

Okay, here we go, I thought. Don't breathe, Paul. Here's where Raymond turns back into his real self again. We're not at Trini's shop so he won't have to act all nice anymore.

I looked through the van's window. Nothing seemed different in there. I pulled the door open, took one deep breath, and climbed in. Before I could even let the breath out, Raymond turned to me and frowned.

Here it comes, I thought, getting ready for whatever torture Ray had planned for me.

"Seat belt on, Paul."

I started breathing normal again and reached for the seat belt. Ray started the engine. Right then I knew something was definitely different inside the van. The awful smells had turned themselves into regular old-car smells.

"It's not too smelly in here," I said to Raymond without thinking. Oh, great! I told myself. You're off to a great start. This is where Raymond whips his arm over and whams you across the chest.

But like when we were in the shop, Raymond just laughed. "Me and the guys were used to it, I guess. Trini never said anything, either. But then last week, she got in, fished around in her tote bag, and pulled out this can of spray—deodorizer or something—and went wild.

"She sprayed under the glove compartment, sprayed my shoes, turned around on the seat and sprayed as far as she could in back. She must've used the whole can before she put the lid on and stuck it back in her bag."

Ray gave me a sorta helpless look. "Neva say one word, uh? Das how dis girl operates. Nex morning I spend bout tree hours cleaning in here, uh?"

I was grinning. Couldn't help myself. Yeah. This sounded more like the old Raymond, back to pidgin again. "Smell like flowers all ova," I said.

"Yeah. Mainland-kine. Lilacs? Trini get perfume—smell like dat."

We'd started up the hill, and even though something in me still waited for Raymond to drop this act and go back to being mean, I decided that Trini must've sprayed away some of the old Raymond, and I could breathe pretty good again.

Raymond switched on his CD player kinda loud then, and we didn't talk until we were in Sal's driveway. I was hoping that Sal would come out of his house when Raymond was putting the Salvadors' bag by their carport door, but nobody came out. I wanted to see Sal's face when he saw me with his brother. Then I felt bad. Maybe Sal was really, really sick and was in bed back there in his bedroom. I'd call him as soon as I got home, I decided.

Raymond climbed back in the driver's seat. "I gotta move, kid," he said, looking at the little digital clock he'd stuck on the van's real clock that didn't work. "No nice little visits for tea and crumpets here or at your house. I'll just dump you off, okay?" He craned his neck back and reversed us down the driveway.

"Sure. You've gotta get to work? You said something about—"

"Oh, yeah. Not really work, yet. More like school. The carpenters' apprenticeship program at the community college. Getting work in this town is almost impossible, believe me."

"Yeah. I know," I said. Pages of newspaper ads squirmed around in my brain. Boy, did I know about finding jobs.

"Except for carpenters, though, did you know that, Paul? People can't afford new houses nowadays, so they're redoing the old ones. Or adding on. They need builders, carpenters, roofers, electricians.

"Trouble is, you can't just run around with a hammer and call yourself a carpenter. You need training. So that's what I'm doing. They work my tail off with carpentry stuff at night, then I've got regular classes in the mornings. After that I put in three more hours playing janitor there to get free tuition and earn some money."

He didn't talk for a minute, and I didn't either. I was trying to make sure this was Raymond Salvador making all these good plans. "What about your birds?" I asked. "You still have the roosters for making money, right?"

He pointed his thumb to the back, behind our seats. "Smell that, Paul?"

"Smell what?"

"That's what I'm talking about. No roosters in here for a while. No time, das why."

I knew I was crazy, but I actually believed him. I stood there by my oranges until his van was kicking up dust down on the road and hoped that things would work out for him and he'd be a carpenter.

I could hardly believe I was wanting good things to happen for Raymond Jesus Salvador!

TWENTY-NINE

After I lugged the oranges into our pantry I did call Sal, and he was feeling better. His voice didn't even sound scratchy. "Too bad," he said. "I could've stayed home and been lazy tomorrow. But I'll probably be fine. Anyways, did you get your tires and stuff?"

"Yeah. I'm all set with the bike."

"Anything else interesting?"

"Ummm...not much." I wasn't really ready to talk about Raymond yet, so we just yakked till Sal yawned and said his mom had told him to rest.

Sal was right—the next morning he wasn't germy so he didn't get to skip school. When his mom came by for us, Em climbed into the very back and I slid in next to Sal. Mom sat in the front with Mrs. Salvador. I was looking out the window at Mr. Freitas's fence when I heard Mom say, "Thanks so much for the oranges, Mona. Those aren't from your old tree, are they?"

"Oranges? Oh. You got oranges, too? I was going to thank *you* for them. You know, Raymond might have dropped those off. He brought us a bunch a couple of weeks ago and said he might get more from his friend."

"If he did, please tell him thanks for us. They're luscious. I had two for breakfast. What a nice thing for him to do…" I could tell Mom was trying not to act surprised. Or maybe she thought Ray was stealing somebody's oranges!

I opened my mouth to say what happened yesterday, about the oranges and Ray taking me home, but then Mrs. S. leaned closer to Mom and said, "You're not going to believe this, Julie, but it looks like Raymond might be getting married!"

"Raymond?" Mom asked. "*Your* Raymond?"

"Our Raymond! Our tough, snarly, don't-need-nobody Raymond. You could have knocked me over with a feather when I heard. I got a call last night, and it was a little late and I was afraid it was bad news. You know how that is when it's dark and the phone rings. But it was Trini Mendoza. She said Raymond came over for a late dinner, and he asked her."

"Oh, for heavens' sake! But did you say Raymond *might* be getting married?"

"Uh-huh. He proposed, but Trini hasn't said yes. I hope she does, though. I like that girl. And I know for sure that she's having a good influence on Ray."

"Better than his little gang, huh?"

"You might not believe this either, but I think Ray's finally starting to outgrow them. He's still living at Roger's, of course, but he's stopped by the house three times in the last week. Make that four if he brought the oranges. He even mumbled a sort of apology to Art for…you know. What I told you?"

Mrs. S. glanced back to see if anybody was listening, and I

acted like I was digging something out of my backpack. In a quieter voice, she said, "I mean that awful fight he had with Art before he moved out. Well, he admitted to his father that he didn't mean most of what he said."

She slowed for the morning traffic, then she said, "Ray always invents an excuse for coming home, of course. He wanted to loan his old surfboard to a friend, he needed to pick up an extra rooster cage, things like that. But at least he's coming. And sometimes even talking."

Mom nodded. "Has he talked with you about Trini?"

"Oh, he's not communicating that much yet! He's still feeling his way along, and this is new territory for him."

Emily poked me in the back of my neck and I batted her hand away. She'd been listening, too. "You guys know Trini, right?" she whispered to me and Sal. "Is she gonna say yes and get married to Raymond?"

"Beats me," Sal said. "Ask my mom." Then, before Em could ask, he said, "Mom? Is this supposed to be a big secret? We were listening back here, you know."

"Ray didn't say anything about it being a secret. I'm sure it's okay."

"So Mrs. Salvador," Emmie said, leaning over the back of my seat so she wouldn't have to yell, "is Trini going to marry him?"

Mrs. S. signaled to turn right onto Kawailoa, the street our school was on. "Don't know, Emily. But she says she's thinking about it. She's noticed some changes in Ray lately, too. Otherwise I'm sure she'd never even think twice about his proposal, even though she says she loves him."

"Cool!" Em said. "Maybe they'll have a baby and you'll be an uncle, Sal."

I pushed Emily's head back and said, "Quit acting like such a...such a *girl*, Emily, and quit breathing on my neck."

"Don't listen to him, Em," Mom said. "This isn't just gossip here. It looks like things are starting to turn around for Raymond, and I for one am really happy about that."

* * *

Sal's mom wasn't waiting for us after school. Emmy was standing by the curb with some of her fellow first-graders, talking away. Sal yelled over to her, "So where's our ride, Emily Cremmily?" She stopped talking and looked up the street, then back at Sal and me, and shrugged her shoulders.

"She'll be here, Sal," I said. "In a minute."

But she wasn't. Not for about ten minutes, and then...oh, man! What I heard—and then what I saw chugging into the school parking lot—was an old green VW van. I couldn't believe it, but it was Raymond all alone in there.

He pulled up right by us and cranked down the passenger side window.

"Anybody here doesn't wanna walk home?" he said, sounding just as friendly as when we were at Trini's and when he drove me home.

Emily picked up her backpack and headed right over. Sal followed her, slid the door open, and hiked her up into the van. He looked back at me just standing there and said, "You walking, Paulie?"

I got in back with Em, and we sat on the floor. Sal crawled into the passenger seat up front.

"Seat belt, Sal," Ray commanded.

Sal looked at him and then, from between the seats, he gave me a quick who-is-this-guy? kind of face. After the seat belt clicked, Raymond put the van in gear. I waited for him to gun the motor a couple of times so the exhaust smoke would make Emily's friends cough and glare at us from the sidewalk, but he just headed out of the driveway, looking both ways before he pulled onto Kawailoa.

"So," Sal said to his brother. "You're not Mom."

Here it goes, I said to myself. The true test. Ray's gonna tell Sal that was a stupid thing to say. I was sure Sal expected that, too, but Ray just said, "I don't look like her? Hmmm…must be the beard." He turned toward Sal and sorta stroked this invisible beard. "Like it? Only one week, uh, and one foot long. Get all nice already."

"Yeah, nice. Lots nicer than Mom's beard…but what I meant was, how come you're here and not Mom or Mrs. Silva?"

"Da muddas? Drive up da mountain to pick up food for da church luau tonight. Get some of da food from dat Yamaguchi place, and da stuff for da tables, den was coming down and one giant mango tree fall, wham!"

"Fell on them? Fell on the car?" Sal sounded as panicked as I was.

"Nah, nah. Jus fell da road." He geared down and then, sounding like he was a completely different person, he said slowly, "The tree fell onto the road and blocked both lanes, so our mothers are still up there waiting for the road to be cleared. The food's all iced in big chests, so it's okay. Everybody's okay." He laughed to himself, or at himself, then finished, "The mango tree's a goner, though! Maybe they'll have mangos for dessert at the luau. God's way of helping out his church, huh?"

Sal nodded. "So Mom had her new cell and she phoned...*you?"*

Raymond laughed again. "Of course she phoned me. After calling maybe sixty other people who weren't home or couldn't get here. So, last resort, she called me. I just happened to be free and...'Raymond to the Rescue!'"

"Ah. That's good, I guess."

They didn't talk again until Ray started up the hill. Then Sal finally asked the question I knew he'd been wondering about. "Why are you acting so nice and talking so funny right now, Ray?"

"Funny? Who, me? Or should I say whom?"

"That's what I mean. Funny. Different. Correct English. You hardly ever talk like this."

"Guess I'm just having fun using one of my many talents. You have no idea how talented your elder brother is, *Angel* Salvador."

THIRTY

I couldn't believe it was Friday afternoon already. I'd told Sal about Ray being nice to me at Trini's and driving me home. I'd told him about Dad's job offer at Mauna Kai Fresh Eggs, too, but not about the rest. I knew I needed to talk with him about not being next-door neighbors pretty soon because of Dad's job—but when he said maybe I could come over after dinner, I said no. "Got lots to do tonight, so I'd better not. I'll hike over in the morning, okay?"

When I got home, I headed straight for the computer. What I'd said about having lots of stuff to do wasn't quite true, but I really wanted to give the "Help Wanted" websites one last try. I kept getting this feeling that maybe I could still find something.

But after about two hours of tracking down one job after another…absolutely nothing. The site might as well have posted a big "No Help Wanted, Any Place, Any Time" banner across its home page.

When I shut down the computer, I felt totally wiped out. After dinner I took a shower and crawled into bed way earlier than usual. That feeling about being able to change things? Just wishful thinking, as my mom would say. Hope's a good thing, but I had to start getting real.

* * *

When I opened my eyes the next morning, I knew from the sun in my window and the fact that no roosters were crowing that it was late. My first thought was that I'd slept in and was late for school, then I remembered it was Saturday, so that was okay. Then I thought…Saturday! It's almost time.

I had to admit to myself that there'd been lots of times when I wanted to get out of the decision I'd made about moving. All last week a big part of me wanted Dad to come over and say, "I'm sorry, son, but we're going to have to stay here and raise roosters for a while longer. Your mom and I appreciate your willingness to help with this, but this is not the alternative we've been searching for."

But then I'd remember telling Dad that I'd be okay with the changes we'd have to make, as long as we could get away from the rooster business. And I knew it was true, what I'd told him and what I'd told Honey. I hated leaving our farm on the mountain, leaving the house where I'd been so happy, but I'd find the good things about the new place. Living downtown would put me within a couple of minutes' walk to the movies. No more waiting for the bus, or having that long bike ride wherever I went. Em and I would stay at the same school, and I'd still see my friends, so at least that much would be just the same. I'd be able to visit Milo at Honey's house.

Best of all, I'd be able to look at roosters again without feeling guilty and sick.

After I had a bowl of cereal—and one of Raymond's famous oranges—I walked over to Sal's.

He was in his carport working on his bike. While I helped him, I told him everything that had gone on during the week.

He hardly said anything, just kept on working and not looking at me, but I could tell he wasn't very happy. Not as upset as Honey, but he was thinking about it. If I moved, it would make things different for him, too. When I'd finished talking, he said he could see why I had to go. That made me feel good. I wasn't sure he'd understand why the rooster thing was so important to me.

"I can take Milo for you if he can't live in the condo," he said, as he picked up his tools.

"You're too late. I already had an offer."

He looked up at me. "Who?"

"Honey."

"So you told her before you even told me? Geez! So much for being your best friend. Hey. Is that who you were with instead of being in the caf yesterday?"

"Yeah. Don't be jealous."

"Yeah, sure. Jealous. That must be it."

We decided to meet at the pond after he was done with his bike and a couple of chores his mom wanted him to do, so I went back home, changed, and grabbed my beach towel.

When I got to our pond, the water had never felt so cool and soft. Sal got there a few minutes after I did. He jumped in and we swam around a while without talking. The sun was warm. We got out and dried off. "You can still come here, you know," Sal said when we were getting some rays. "It'll still be here. You'll just have to come on up the hill."

"Sure. I know that. Guess I'm just sad because it won't be so easy to come over and bug you anymore."

"Yeah. I'll have to call Ray and have him come back and bug me…wait! I didn't tell you. Ray's gonna marry Trini. Or Trini's gonna marry *him.* In a couple of months. A real wedding at St. Ann's."

"He told you guys? Or did your mom talk to Trini again?"

"Nope. Raymond called, himself, right before I came up here. Mom about went crazy when she heard the news. She said Ray and Trini went down to the beach for an early morning swim today and had this really long talk, and she decided to say yes. Ray put Trini on the line and she and my mom talked about wedding stuff—flowers, dresses—I don't remember what all.

"But anyways, everybody's happy and crazy. Ray's looking for some real work, and they're gonna live at Trini's apartment until they can get a house. My stupid brother. Can you imagine anybody wanting to marry him?"

"Well, not the *old* Raymond," I said.

Sal asked me why I had this weird look on my face but I knew I'd never tell him. The lava rock was something just between me and Raymond Salvador.

THIRTY-ONE

After the pond, Sal had to go home, and I went to the infirmary. Dad and Porky were off someplace, so I fussed around for a while, cleaning up and making sure everything was back together again from the experiment. Dad's new chicks were four days old, already feathery and funny. I watched them waddle around and bump into each other and look for food.

When I went back up to my room, I wondered what I could do to waste some time and I decided to check out stuff on roosters on my computer. It would be more fun now, because it wouldn't be for a school project anymore. Well...it might be—I might get an idea for a really challenging topic to experiment with next year. Something so cool Mrs. Chong and Mr. Miyagi would send me over to Honolulu for the regionals. Then, of course, to the national competition.

"First Place in the Universe Science Fair goes to...Paul Allan Silva!"

I Googled some rooster sites. Learned that all the domestic roosters came from this wild Red Jungle Fowl who lived in

Asia. Found out that scientists were studying the wild roosters that were still left. I couldn't believe it when I read one of their conclusions: roosters don't like to fight.

I read part of a long study of feral chickens done by some scientist in Australia. A couple of sentences jumped right out at me: "No serious fights were observed. Instead, the cocks showed only protective behavior toward the hens, and fought each other only at the times when they thought their hens were being attacked."

So much for Sal's big idea that fighting was in the roosters' genes. I went to some other sites, just to have something to do. To keep myself from thinking about everything that was going to happen.

An article called "Chickens Are Foragers, Not Fighters" said pretty much the same thing as the first one I read. Another study was about whether roosters feel pain. That was a no-brainer. Of course they do! I didn't need researchers to tell me that if you pinch a chicken's comb he'll squawk. Birds feel real pain, just the way other animals and people do. Another article said that chickens were at least as smart as dogs. I'd known that for a long time, too, but it was good having scientists say I was right.

I clicked on one site after another and wondered why I hadn't really looked at all this stuff before we started our project. I was getting tons of ideas for next year's project.

But when I clicked on this link called "rooster behavior studies," something totally wild happened.

A bunch of sites appeared on the screen, and right near the top of the list were two or three about rescuing fighting cocks. I'd never even thought there might be people out there trying to save roosters.

I read one of the papers and I couldn't believe it. It wasn't just about rescuing roosters after the cockfights and putting them in shelters. Not just about stitching them up and being kind to them. These people were *retraining* them! They were teaching them how to be normal roosters again. Making it safe for them to be around other roosters, and letting them take care of their hens the way the birds do when nobody teaches them they're supposed to fight.

I read more and more articles. If what I was reading was true, this wasn't just a crazy idea. It was going on in lots of different places. People weren't just working with these birds and keeping them in a safe place, they were figuring out cool ways to rehabilitate them. The retraining was working, and the people who were doing it were called scientific pioneers.

After about an hour of reading online, I wrote down the phone numbers from three of the websites. I looked at my watch. I would need to hurry.

All the numbers were on the mainland. The first one was on the East Coast. They were six hours ahead of us and I couldn't call there this late. The other two numbers were on the West Coast, only three hours ahead, even with daylight savings time, which we don't have in Hawaii. It was Saturday, but I might be able to reach somebody.

I jumped up and when I found Mom in the kitchen I asked her, "Can I use the phone card, Mom? I've gotta phone somebody long distance."

"It's important?"

"Really, *really* important. I hafta call right now."

"Okay then. Go ahead. Just let me know when you decide to share the big mystery."

I ran back into Dad's office, took the blue-and-orange card out of the desk drawer, and grabbed the phone. I dialed all the numbers on the card and then the number of the California scientist who worked with roosters. No answer. Not even an answering machine. I tried again just in case I hadn't dialed it right, but no luck.

Only one number left, of a scientist who lived in Oregon. Her name was Dr. Elizabeth Madden. I punched in the numbers, careful not to miss one. I heard a ring.

"Hello," a lady's voice said.

Somebody was home!

"Um, hello," I said. "Is this Dr. Madden?"

"Speaking. How can I help you?"

She sounded nice. And she let me talk. I told her who I was and where I lived and what I'd read and everything, and she listened and didn't interrupt when I had to take breaths or think of what to say next. Then, finally, I stopped.

"You're how old, Paul?" she wanted to know. When I said I was almost thirteen, I thought she might hang up on me, or at least make me bring my parents in to talk with her, but she didn't. She was quiet for a while, but I knew she hadn't hung up. I could hear chicken sounds on her phone.

"Listen, Paul," she said, "can you hold on for a minute until I walk over to my office? You got me on my cell phone. I'm here at the shelter right now, out with the roosters. I just have to put the phone down for a second and lock up this area for today. Is that okay? This is long distance for you—do you need for me to call you back when I get in the building?"

I said, no, I had a phone card so she didn't need to call me back. It wasn't expensive. Then I waited, trying to be patient. I put my head back and stretched my neck. Then my arms, one at a time, clamping the phone between my ear and my shoulder. I looked at my watch about a hundred times, but it clicked to a new minute only two times. It just *seemed* like an hour.

Finally I heard her say, "Paul? You're still there?"

"Yes, Dr. Madden."

"I'm in an old barn now. We were given this farm, and we restored the great old barn and turned it into offices. We use this little one I'm in now, then we rent out the others to nonprofit organizations. There. I've booted up my computer."

Dr. Madden told me more about the organization she worked for and gave me some more websites and phone numbers to write down. Then she asked me a ton of questions: what our farm was like, how many roosters we had, things like that.

Then she didn't talk for a minute and I got worried again that she might hang up, but before I about went crazy she said, "I've read that cockfighting is big in Hawaii. Is that correct, Paul?"

"You wouldn't believe it. Especially on this island."

Then I told her more about our A-frame rooster hutches and the infirmary and she said, "Wow! Paul Silva, it sounds like you're living on the ideal site for a rooster sanctuary. I'm really impressed."

I was getting impressed, too, but then it hit me. Tomorrow Dad had to give his answer to Mr. Fernandez. There was no time to figure out something new. And I had to be honest with Dr. Madden.

"We're gonna have to move away from here, though," I told her. "Probably soon."

And I told her all the rest, then. About the alternative job thing. Everything. Well, everything except about Milo, because I wasn't sure a scientist would understand about that.

"Paul," her nice voice said then, "I may be able to help you out with this. I can just say 'may' at this point, so please don't get your hopes up too high. I need to talk with some people before I can make any promises to you. That's because I'm not the boss on this project, you understand?"

"Yes. No promises right now."

"But I have your phone number, and I *can* promise that I'll call you back tomorrow, no matter what happens. When would be a good time? And would your father be available? I'll need to talk to him, too."

Quick, I figured out when we'd be home from church in the morning—around eleven o'clock, Hawaii time. Two in the afternoon, Oregon time. I asked her if 2:15 in the afternoon would be good, and she said it would be fine. She'd need some time to consult with the other board members. I told her my dad would be home then, and we were saying goodbye when she said something that made me feel hopeful.

"Okay, then, Paul," she said. "And I thank you so much."

"For what, Dr. Madden?"

"For calling. For caring and trying. This is how we'll make the world better, you know. Better for people and animals. One rooster at a time, Paul. That's what it will take."

I tried to keep calm when I hung up the phone, but I was so excited that I was ready to go and tell Dad everything that very second! I couldn't wait to run in and tell Mom. To tell Emily and Milo and Sal and Honey and the whole world!

But then I reminded myself that this might be too good to be true. Dr. Madden said not to get my hopes up too high. So I forced myself to calm down. Took deep breaths. Milo wandered in and I didn't tell him anything. Just tossed his squeaky mouse toy around and watched him pounce on it a few times. Tried not to think that we might be safe and that I might not need to give him to Honey.

So when Dad came in and asked when I was going to tell him about the mystery phone call my mom told him about, I just said, "Tomorrow."

THIRTY-TWO

I couldn't tell what woke me up. Was it sounds of roosters or smells of cinnamon rolls baking? Before I was awake enough to figure that out, to remember that it was Sunday and maybe the most important day of all my life, I just sniffed and listened, and let myself be happy.

It had probably been the smell that woke me up, I decided. Sometimes Mom made us cinnamon rolls with part of her Portuguese sweet bread dough. She let Emily help her roll the dough out, brush it with melted butter, and sprinkle it with cinnamon and brown sugar. They rolled it up, sliced it, and put the little pinwheels in a round pan. Some were baking now, and oh, they smelled so great!

Or it might have been our roosters singing. It was kind of a silly thought—who would ever think that roosters could make a song? But they seemed to be excited today. Not wild-boar excited or getting-stolen excited, just singing-about-the-morning-together excited, kinda like I felt.

I was wound up in Auntie Sylvana's quilt like a long roll of cinnamon rolls ready to be sliced into pieces, so I let go of the end of the quilt and unrolled myself. In just a little while I was dressed in good jeans and my best blue aloha shirt, the one with white *pikake* leis printed on it, and almost ready for church.

"Portuguese sausage and scrambled eggs," Dad said when I went into the kitchen. He hadn't looked up from making them, but he knew I was there.

"And *cinnamon rolls!*" said Em. "I made them."

"You didn't make the dough, Cremmily," I said.

"No, but I made the cinnamon rolls and they're going to be delicious, Paul, so don't act so smart."

I sat down at the table. Mom opened the oven door and even more smell steamed out into the kitchen before she closed it. "Five minutes, Art," she said, and Dad nodded.

I watched them work together and for some reason I remembered that I'd fallen asleep in the middle of my prayers last night. I was trying to make God figure out if I should tell Mom and Dad about my Dr. Madden secret or just surprise them if the news was good. Maybe I got an answer, because when we were eating, I looked at Dad's face, then Mom's and Emily's, and I started telling them. They had to know. It wasn't just a Paul thing now.

Emily still hadn't been told about moving, so I was careful. I explained about rooster shelters and who Dr. Madden was and what we'd talked about. Mom and Emily asked me a couple of questions, but Dad didn't say anything until I was finished, and then he said, "Good heavens, Paul. What have you been up to? Are you going to be running all our lives from now on?"

"Um, no. I mean, this might not happen and if it does, you don't have to do it if you don't want to, but I thought if it did happen you would be happy and—"

I felt Dad's hand on my arm and I stopped talking and looked at his face. It was okay, I knew then. All of it. He was smiling, and even when he said, "It would be pleasant if, just for once, you'd tell your parents what you're up to," I knew I hadn't done anything terrible.

Then Emily changed the subject to could she go home from church with Ariel for lunch, found out it was okay, and leaned back in her chair looking happy. She unwound her second cinnamon roll and ate it bite by bite until she got to the middle. I didn't give her a hard time about it because that's how I eat cinnamon rolls, too.

It had been a good idea, I decided, not telling Emmy about moving. When she's a little bit older, we won't be able to protect her from things, but now we can. There are good things about being a little kid.

"Your cinnamon rolls are delicious, Emily," I told her.

She said, "I *told* you, Paul."

Mom looked at me and said, "Yes, your sister's becoming an excellent baker." She scooted her chair back and stood up. "And now you guys need to take care of these dishes for me while I get ready. We can finish cleaning up when we get home, but just rinse things off so those little black ants don't find them while we're gone. They come in through the window screen and they're driving me crazy."

We did rinse off the dishes, and in about ten minutes we were heading down to St. Ann's.

I had lots of trouble listening to Father Randy, this young priest we just got at St. Ann's. My mind kept running from this thought over to that one. I didn't fall asleep in the prayers like I did last night, but I kept praying that Dr. Madden would have good news and then worrying that I was being selfish and making God mad.

Then when I tuned Father Randy back in, he said something that made me glad I'd come.

"Don't worry about the *quality* of your prayers," he was saying. "God loves you and knows you're not perfect, so *he* doesn't worry. He wants you to be able to talk with him whenever you can."

It was good that we had church today. If we hadn't, I think I'd have gone crazy. We got home a little before eleven, twenty minutes before Dr. Madden was supposed to call. It seemed like a hundred hours.

I didn't change into my old clothes, and when I went in to help Mom finish cleaning up the kitchen, she put an apron on me so I wouldn't get stuff on my good shirt. I was starting to complain about that when the wall phone rang and I grabbed it with my soapy hands...but it was just Em phoning from Ariel's saying to tell Mom that Ariel's mom would bring her home around three.

"Okay, okay, Emily. I've got it," I said. "I'm waiting for a real phone call, you know."

"Well, ex*cuse* me," she said, and hung up.

"Go," Mom said. "That wasn't very nice, and you're doing a lousy job in here. Go and wait in your dad's office." She turned her head to look at me and her face changed to smiling. "And you can take off my frilly little apron before you go. Even though it looks very pretty on you!"

So I did what she said and plunked down on Dad's office chair. Finally it was 11:15. And the phone didn't ring. Eleven seventeen. She was late. How could she be late? Didn't we decide on 11:15? And now it was almost 11:20.

I picked up Milo's mouse and his stuffed toad and tried to juggle them. Then I whirled the mouse around and around until its long tail wound around my finger. I was trying to use it like a mouse yo-yo when Dad came in and said, "Put that thing down, Paul. It's not very sanitary, you know."

"But Dad. It's after"—I looked at my watch—"after eleven-twenty-*three!*"

"From what you've told me, Paul, it sounds like your Dr. Madden will call, one way or the other."

"But you know what this means? The people on the committee, on the board, or whatever, the people who have to decide…they said no and she doesn't want to tell us."

"It means nothing of the sort. Now tell you what. You go in the kitchen. Look out the window. Pace the floor, if you know how to do that. When the kitchen phone rings, answer it. I'll let you talk for a few minutes, then I'll listen in here and if she wants to talk to me—"

RRRIINNGG!

I stood there staring at the phone.

"Pick it up, Paul."

I did. And after I said a shaky "hello," I heard her voice saying, "Paul? Elizabeth Madden here. Are you there?"

I said yes in kind of a high voice, then I cleared my throat and said it again.

"I'm sorry we're a few minutes late," she said, "but you're talking with three of us. Andrew Pribilsky and Marion Atwater are on the line. They're part of the Foundation's board of directors, and they wanted to talk with you, so it took us a minute to set up a conference call. Marion's in Texas and Andrew's in Montana."

A lady and a man said hello, and I said hello and then *finally* Dr. Madden said what I'd waited forever to hear.

"Paul, we've been researching other places where we might set up more sanctuaries, and Hawaii is a likely location. A friend of Marion's who now lives in Honolulu has been looking for an opportunity like this, and he's very interested in helping us out. We'll need to confirm the funding with the rest of the board, but things are looking good."

"Looking good? Looking good?" Those were the only words I could understand right then, so I repeated them. Twice.

"Yes, Paul," the man's voice said, and I heard the three people laugh, and I looked at Dad and he even laughed and shook his head like he couldn't believe it.

Looking good. I listened to Dr. Madden and the board people but all I could think of was, Yes! The roosters will be safe. Yes! Dad will have a job he loves. We won't have to move. I can keep my promises.

After a few minutes, Dr. Madden asked if my father could come to the phone, and I think I said thank you a dozen times before I said sure, he's right here, and handed the phone over to him. Then I collapsed in his desk chair while he listened and then said things like, "It's nice talking with all of you," and "Yes, he explained things to his mother and me this morning, when he was a little more coherent than he is now!" and "What a wonderful possibility this is."

And after a while, he said, "That would definitely cover our expenses, Dr. Madden.... Yes, I understand. The Foundation would need to inspect our property. To provide special training for me, and possibly for my brother. I'll approach him with the idea. A lot has to be done of course..."

I could tell that Dad was repeating things so I could hear them, too. I could have gone in the kitchen and listened in, but I liked it better this way.

"Your sponsors sound committed to this, Dr. Madden.... Yes. The future." He listened some more then said, "Not quite thirteen, but he cares deeply about this.... Yes. The children. They're the ones who will make a difference."

He talked some more and then he said goodbye and mahalo. After he'd hung up the phone, he just stared at it for a minute. Then he looked at me for the first time since he'd started talking. He had a bigger grin on his face than I'd seen anytime since before that awful day at Nakasone's Lumber Company when he left work in the ambulance. I knew he wouldn't yell or cheer or say anything sappy, but that smile told me everything.

"Well, Paul," he said in a calm voice. "You've been listening to my side of the conversation for about twenty minutes here. I guess you'll want to listen to this next one, too. I'm thinking about calling Matt Fernandez."

"Yeah. I really want to hear this one, too."

He reached in the drawer and took out the sheet of paper where he'd written Eggie's dad's number. "Wow," he said, shaking his head. "I don't know how you pulled this off, Paul, but we didn't have much more time. You might've come up with this alternative employment sooner, right? To keep me from almost having a nervous breakdown?"

I went over and put my arm around his shoulders. Then I looked at the piece of paper he'd pulled out of the drawer. I dialed the number and when I heard a man's voice, I handed Dad the phone.

"Matt?" Dad said. "Hey, Art Silva here.... Yeah. Fine. Everything's great here. Say, I really appreciate your thinking of me for the job, but it looks like my son, here, has already found one for me. I'll tell you about it later.... Yeah. Paul. So you're welcome to put the ad in the *Shoreline*.... Yeah. Thanks again. It was good to know somebody else had confidence in me at this point, Matt.... Sure. See ya around. I'll buy you coffee, okay?"

After he hung up we just looked at each other for a second without saying anything.

"Well, Paul, would you also like to come along with me to tell your mom what's happening with this scheme you cooked up?"

"Sure," I said. "Why not, uh?"

But that very second, Mom ran in saying, "Yes, yes, *yes,* you guys! This is so, so great!" She grabbed me and hugged me, then got her arms around Dad, too, and we were all hugging each other until Dad pulled us off of him. "Julie, you big cheat," he said. "You listened on the kitchen phone, didn't you?"

"Of course I did. This isn't just a man's thing, you know. Just ask Dr. *Elizabeth* Madden!"

THIRTY-THREE

It took us all a long time to calm down. When I'd come back to walking on the ground again I realized that I just had to tell Sal. I hadn't said a thing last night when I came up with the crazy idea, but today…I knew!

But I couldn't just phone him. I ran over. Mrs. S. took one look at me, panting away, and pointed to Sal's room.

I slowed down in the hallway enough to see that her picture of *The Last Supper* was back on the wall. No broken glass. No terrible troubles with Raymond here anymore. Sal's house was all peaceful again.

Sal was relaxing on his bed, but not for long. I dived on him, and we both bounced until he got himself out from under me.

"Hey, Paul! Have you gone crazy?"

"Nope. But *you* will when I tell you what happened!"

I did, and he definitely went crazy! He was laughing and yelling.

"Oh, man! I really, really didn't want you to move, Paulie. I tried to act cool so you wouldn't feel worse, but I felt awful.

And I'm surprised about the shelter thing—who knew there were rooster rescuers out there? My grampa's not going to believe all of this."

"I can't believe it either, neighbor."

When I left, Sal walked me down to the road, even though I told him I knew the way. "I better go with you," he said. "You might trip and fall on your okole."

It was almost time for Honey to come when I got back home. I still had on my good church aloha shirt, and I brushed my hair. Then I sat on the porch swing on our front lanai, waiting for Mr. Kealoha's blue truck to turn into our driveway. I wanted to look casual, so I propped my feet up on the railing, but in a while they started to get all prickly and go to sleep, so then I stuck them back down in my rubber slippers.

Old Milo hopped up on my lap and turned over on his back for me to scratch his white chest, his favorite place to get scratched.

"Hey, stupid cat," I said to him. "Guess what. We're not moving!" He just yawned in my face, then after he got all the petting he wanted, he flipped back over and jumped off of my lap.

"You don't know how close you came to being Honey Kealoha's cat!" I yelled after him. "You'd have hated it there. She'd forget to feed you and she sure wouldn't spend all her time scratching your chest!"

I looked at my watch. Two minutes after one. Oh, man, I hoped she didn't forget! This time I *didn't* want the phone to ring because it might be Honey saying she couldn't come.

This was twice today I was looking at the time and waiting, and I knew I just had to learn to be patient.

Another five minutes. Maybe I should go inside so I didn't look like I was waiting for her when she came. No, I'd give her five more minutes.

One minute later the truck pulled up. Honey hopped down, and after she'd waved thanks to her dad, he threw the truck in reverse and backed down to the road.

I stayed on the lanai porch, but I stood up. We said "Hi" and stuff, then we went into the kitchen for a few minutes. I tried to not look too happy and give everything away, but it was hard. I wanted to tell her that very second everything that had happened.

But Honey got busy talking to Mom, telling her how beautiful her new wreaths looked. Mom said I'd helped on those, and Honey looked at me like she couldn't believe it.

"These are your own woodroses, Mrs. Silva?" Honey asked. "All of them? The big ones and the cute little ones, all of them grew up here on the hill?"

Mom nodded. "Paul can show you where the vines grow. Out in back by the bamboo grove. You two don't have to stay here and keep me company, you know. Grab a soda or some juice. Or a cinnamon roll. Fresh-baked today."

"Ah," Honey said. "I thought I smelled cinnamon rolls. I absolutely love them."

"We'll take two, okay?" I said to Mom.

We carried our cranberry-orange drinks and our rolls out back, and after I pointed to where the woodroses grew, we sat down across from each other at the picnic table. I decided I had to tell her right then. That very second. But before I could open my mouth, she reached her hand across the table and covered my hand with hers. And all of a sudden I had no idea what I'd been planning to say.

"So, Paul Silva," she said. "Let's start all over again. That's what I really wanted to tell you on Friday. I really do like you, you know."

She slid her other hand under my fingers, and my hand felt warm between them. I wanted everything to stay like that forever. Feeling Honey's hands holding onto mine. Sitting here with her by the tree ferns and the tall green bamboo. And best of all, I thought, hearing that she liked me and knowing I liked her, too.

I shook my head to get the dreams out of it, then I smoothed my hair down. When I felt her pull her hands back, I got brave and I held *her* hands for a minute. I kinda cleared my throat, then I said, "I hated it when I knew something was wrong. We won't be that way again."

"We'll talk, okay?"

"Sure. We can talk about anything you want, you know. Not just about me all the time. We can talk about your mom if you feel like it sometime."

She thought about that for a few seconds, then she said, "I'd like that sometime, but not right now. It's still pretty hard for me, and I cry a lot. But later…well, I think I'd like that." She looked around her. "For now, we can talk about 'here,' maybe. It's beautiful here, Paul, and I'm so, so sorry that you'll have to…"

And that's when I told her we'd be able to stay, and what

we'd be doing. I didn't brag or show off or try to get her approval. I'd done that before and it didn't work out so great.

"So when you come up here from now on," I finished, "you won't hafta think about death anymore, okay?"

"Never again. Oh, Paul, this is so absolutely, totally…I don't know what to say!"

In a second, she pulled her legs up under her on the bench and stood on her knees so she could reach farther across the table. She put her hands on my cheeks. Then she leaned way, way over and gave me a kiss. Not on my mouth, just on my forehead, but it was a real kiss, and I wasn't even embarrassed. It was a great kiss, and it came from Honey Kealoha! For a minute, I just kept blinking my eyes. Did it really happen?

"We've talked about enough serious stuff for one day, Paulie." She sat back down, then slid off her bench and stood up. "Come on," she said, and I got up, too.

"Where to?" I asked her when she reached her hand out to me.

"Out in front, Paul. To look at your view of the ocean. And to watch your beautiful roosters."

—End—